T0029057

A SPINDLE
SPLINTERED

TORDOTCOM BOOKS BY ALIX E. HARROW

A Spindle Splintered

A SPINDLE SPLINTERED

Alix E. Harrow

A TOM DOHERTY ASSOCIATES BOOK
NEW YORK

Many silhouette illustrations by Arthur Rackham set throughout this book were unavoidably harmed, fractured, and splintered during the design process. Can you spot the changes?

This is a work of fiction. All of the characters, organizations, and events portrayed in this novel are either products of the author's imagination or are used fictitiously.

A SPINDLE SPLINTERED

Copyright © 2021 by Alix E. Harrow

All rights reserved.

Edited by Jonathan Strahan

Designed by Gregory Collins

Interior illustrations by Arthur Rackham

A Tordotcom Book
Published by Tom Doherty Associates
120 Broadway
New York, NY 10271

www.tor.com

Tor® is a registered trademark of Macmillan Publishing Group, LLC.

The Library of Congress Cataloging-in-Publication Data is available upon request.

ISBN 978-1-250-76535-2 (hardcover)
ISBN 978-1-250-76536-9 (ebook)

Our books may be purchased in bulk for promotional, educational, or business use. Please contact your local bookseller or the Macmillan Corporate and Premium Sales Department at 1-800-221-7945, extension 5442, or by email at MacmillanSpecialMarkets@macmillan.com.

First Edition: October 2021

Printed in the United States of America

0 9 8 7 6 5 4 3 2

for everyone who deserves a better story
than the one they have

1

SLEEPING BEAUTY IS pretty much the worst fairy tale, any way you slice it.

It's aimless and amoral and chauvinist as shit. It's the fairy tale that feminist scholars cite when they want to talk about women's passivity in historical narratives. ("She literally *sleeps* through her own *climax*," as my favorite gender studies professor used to say. "Double entendre *fully* intended."). *Jezebel* ranked it as the "least woke" Disney movie of all time, which, in a world where *The Little Mermaid* exists, is really saying something. Ariel might have given up her voice for a dude, but Aurora barely uses hers: she has a grand total of eighteen (18) lines in her own movie, fewer than the prince, the villain, or any of the individual fairy godmothers.

Even among the other nerds who majored in folklore, Sleeping Beauty is nobody's favorite. Romantic girls like Beauty and the Beast; vanilla girls like Cinderella; goth girls like Snow White.

Only dying girls like Sleeping Beauty.

❦ ❦ ❦

I DON'T REMEMBER the first time I saw *Sleeping Beauty*—probably in some waiting room or hospital bed, interrupted by blipping machines and chirpy nurses—but I remember the first time I saw Arthur Rackham's illustrations. It was my sixth birthday, after cake but before my evening pills. The second-to-last gift was a cloth-bound copy of Grimm's fairy tales from Dad. I was flipping through it (pretending to be a little more excited than I actually was because even at six I knew my parents needed a lot of protecting) when I saw her: a woman in palest watercolor lying artfully across her bed. Eyes closed, one hand dangling white and limp, throat arched. Black-ink shadows looming like crows around her.

She looked beautiful. She looked dead. Later I'd find out that's how every Sleeping Beauty looks—hot and blond and dead, lying in a bed that might be a bier. I touched the curve of her cheek, the white of her palm, half hypnotized.

But I wasn't really a goner until I turned the page. She was still hot and blond but no longer dead. Her eyes were wide open, blue as June, defiantly alive.

And it was like—I don't know. A beacon being lit, a flint being struck in my chest. Charm (Charmaine Baldwin, best/only friend) says Sleeping Beauty was my first crush and she's not totally wrong, but it was more than that. It was like looking into a mirror and seeing my face reflected brighter and better. It was my own shitty story made mythic and grand and beautiful. A princess cursed at birth. A sleep that never ends. A dying girl who refused to die.

Objectively, I'm aware our stories aren't that similar. Wicked fairies are thin on the ground in rural Ohio, and I'm not suffering from a curse so much as fatal teratogenic damage caused by corporate malfeasance. If you drew a Venn diagram between me and Briar Rose, the overlap would be: (1) doomed to die young, (2) hot, in a fragile, consumptive way, (3) named after flowers. (I mean, look: I have a folklore degree. I'm aware that Sleeping Beauty's name has ranged from Talia to Aurora to Zellandine (do *not* Google that last one), but the Grimms called her Briar Rose and my name is Zinnia Gray, so just let me have this one, alright?). I'm not even blond.

After that birthday I was pretty obsessed. It's one of the rules for dying girls: if you like something, like it *hard*, because you don't have a lot of time to waste. So I had Sleeping Beauty bedsheets and Sleeping Beauty toothpaste and Sleeping Beauty Barbies. My bookshelves filled with Grimm and Lang and then McKinley and Levine and Yolen. I read every retelling and every picture book; I bought a DVD set of the original *Alvin and the Chipmunks* run just to watch episode 85B, "The Legend of Sleeping Brittany," which was just as awful as every other chipmunk-related piece of media. By the time I was twelve, I'd seen a thousand beauties prick their fingers on a thousand spindles, a thousand castles swallowed by a thousand rose hedges. I still wanted more.

I graduated high school two years early—another one of the rules for dying girls is *move fast*—and went straight into the Department of Folk Studies and Anthropology at Ohio University. Seven semesters later I had an impractical degree, a two-hundred-page thesis on representations of disability and chronic illness in European folklore, and less than a year left to live.

Dad would cry if he heard me say that. Mom would invent some urgent task in her flower beds, tending things that weren't going to die on her. Charm would roll her eyes and tell me to quit being such a little bitch about it (it takes a particular kind of tough to pick the dying girl to be your best friend).

All of them would remind me that I don't know exactly how long I've got, that Generalized Roseville Malady is still largely unstudied, that new treatments are being tested as we speak, etc., etc., but the fact is that nobody with GRM has made it to twenty-two.

Today is my twenty-first birthday.

My relatives are all over for dinner and my grandma is drinking like a fish, if fish drank scotch, and my worst aunt is badgering Dad about crystals and alternative therapies. My cheeks hurt from fake-smiling and my poor parents are doing their very best to keep the

celebration from feeling like a wake and I have never been more relieved in my short, doomed life to feel the buzz of my phone on my hip. It's Charm, of course: happy birthday!!

And then: meet me at the tower, princess.

❂ ❂ ❂

TOWERS, LIKE WICKED fairies, are pretty rare in Ohio. We mostly have pole barns and Jesus-y billboards and endless squares of soybeans. Roseville has a tower, though. There's an old state penitentiary out on Route 32, abandoned in the '60s or '70s. Most of it is hulking brick buildings with smashed-out windows and mediocre graffiti, obviously haunted, but there's an old watchtower standing on one corner. It should be exactly as creepy as the rest of the place, poisoned by decades of human misery and institutional injustice, but instead it looks . . . lost. Out of time and place, like a landlocked lighthouse. Like a fairy tale tower somehow washed up on the shores of the real world.

It's where I always planned to die, in my morbid preteen phase. I imagined I would dramatically rip the IVs from my veins and limp down the county road, suffocating in my own treacherous proteins, collapsing Gothic-ly and attractively just as I reached the highest room. My hair would fan into a black halo around the bloodless white of my face and whoever found me would be forced to pause and sigh at the sheer picturesque tragedy of the thing. Eat your heart out, Rackham.

God, middle schoolers are intense. I no longer plan to make anyone discover my wasted body, because I'm not a monster, but I still visit the tower sometimes. It's where I went after high school to ditch track practice and get high with Charm; it's where I made out for the first time (also with Charm, before I instituted dying girl rule number #3); it's where I go when I can't stand to be in my own house, my own skin, for another second.

I switch off the headlights and coast the last quarter mile down Route 32, because the old penitentiary is technically private property upon which trespassers will be shot, and park in the grass. I pop my eight o'clock handful of pills and make my way down the rutted lane that leads to the old watchtower.

I'm not surprised to see the orange flicker of light in the windows.

I figure Charm dragged a few of our friends—her friends, if we're being honest—out here for a party, rather than hosting it in the hazardous waste zone she calls an apartment. I bet she brought red plastic cups and a half keg because she wants me to have a legit twenty-first-birthday experience, completely ignoring the fact that alcohol interferes with at least three of my meds, because that's the kind of friend she is.

But when I step through the tower door, it doesn't smell like beer and weed and mildew. It smells luxuriant, heady, so sweet I feel like an old-timey cartoon character hooked by the nostrils.

I waft up the staircase. There are murmuring voices above me, faint strains of very un-Charm-like music growing louder. The highest room in the tower has always been empty except for the detritus left by time and teenagers: windblown leaves, beer tabs, cicada shells, a condom or two. It's not empty tonight. There are strings of pearled lights crisscrossing the ceiling and long swaths of blushing fabric draped over the windows; a dozen or so people wearing the kind of gauzy fairy wings that come from the year-round Halloween store at the mall; roses absolutely *everywhere*, bursting from buckets and mason jars and Carlo Rossi jugs. And in the very center of the room, looking dusty and rickety and somehow grand: a spinning wheel.

That's when I recognize the song that's playing: "Once Upon a Dream." The main theme from Disney's *Sleeping Beauty,* a waltzing melody stolen straight from Tchaikovsky's ballet.

I am way, way too old for a Sleeping Beauty–themed birthday. I can't stop smiling. "Oh, *Charm,* you *didn't.*"

"I one hundred percent did." Charm passes her PBR to the girl beside her and flings herself at me. She does a little heel-pop when I hug her, like an actress in a black-and-white movie except with more tattoos and piercings. "Happy birthday, baby, from your fairy godmothers." She waggles her wings at me—blue, because Merryweather is her favorite character—and mashes a plastic princess crown onto my head.

Our friends (her friends) clap and hoot and pass me warmish beer. Someone switches the music, thank God, and for a few hours I pretend I'm just like them. Young and thoughtless and happy, poised at the first chapter of my story instead of the last.

Charm keeps it going as long as she can. She forces everyone into a game of Disney trivia that appears to have no rules except that I always win; she passes around pink-and-blue frosted cupcakes in a plastic Walmart clamshell; she plucks petals from the roses and flings them at me whenever my smile threatens to sag. Everybody seems to enjoy themselves.

For a while.

But there's only so long you can hang out with the dying girl and her best friend without mortality coming to tap her knucklebones at your window. By eleven, somebody gets drunk enough to ask me, "So like, what are you doing this fall?" and a chill slinks into the room. It coils around our ankles and shivers down our spines and suddenly the roses smell like a funeral and nobody is meeting my eyes.

I consider lying. Pretending I have some internship or job or adventure lined up like the rest of them, when really I have nothing planned but a finite number of family game nights, during which my parents will stare tenderly at me across the dining room table and I will slowly suffocate under the terrible weight of their love.

"You know." I shrug. "Just playing out the clock." I try to make it jokey, but I can tell there's too much acid in my voice.

After that, Charm's friends slither out of the tower in cowardly twos and threes until it's just the two of us, like it usually is. Like it won't be for too much longer. Her friends took their speaker with them, so the tower is silent except for the gentle rush of wind against the windows, the crack and hiss of another beer being opened.

Charm resettles her fairy wings and looks over at me with a dangerous softening around her eyes, mouth half open, and I have a terrible premonition that she's about to say something unforgivably sincere, like *I love you* or *I'll miss you.*

I flick my chin at the spinning wheel. "Dare you to prick your finger."

Charm tosses a bleached slice of hair out of her eyes, softness vanishing. "You're the princess, hon." She winks. "But I'll kiss you after." Her voice is saucy but unserious, which is a relief. Dying girl rule #3 is *no romance*, because my entire life is one long trolley problem and I don't want to put any more bodies on the tracks. (I've spent enough time in therapy to know that this isn't "a healthy attitude toward attachment," but I personally feel that accepting my own imminent mortality is enough work without also having a healthy attitude about it.)

"You know it wasn't originally a spinning wheel in the story?" I offer, because alcohol transforms me into a chatty Wikipedia page. "In the original version—I mean, if oral traditions had original versions, which they don't—she pricks her finger on a piece of flax. The Grimms used the word *spindel*, or spindle, but the wheel itself wasn't commonly used in Europe until the mid-sixteenth . . . why are your eyes closed?"

"I'm praying for your amyloidosis to flare up and end my pain."

"Okay, fuck you?"

"Do you have any idea how hard it is to fit a spinning wheel in the trunk of a Corolla? Just prick your finger already! It's almost midnight."

"That's Cinderella, dumbass." But I lurch obediently to my feet, discovering from the delicate spin of the windows that I'm slightly drunker than I'd guessed. I curtsy to Charm, wobble only a little, and touch my finger to the spindle's end.

Nothing happens, naturally. Why would it? It's just a dusty antique in an abandoned watchtower, not nearly sharp enough to draw blood, and I'm just a dying girl with bad luck and a boring life. Neither of us is anything special.

I look down at the iron spike of the spindle, slightly cross-eyed. For no reason I think of the girl in that Rackham illustration, blond and tragic. I think how it must have felt to grow up in the shadow of a curse, how much she must have hated the story she was handed. How in the end all her hate didn't matter because she still reached her finger for that spindle, powerless to stop the cruel gears of her own narrative—

Distantly, I hear Charm say, "Jesus, Zin," and I become aware that I'm pressing my finger into the spindle's end, burying the point in the soft meat of my skin. I look down to see a single red tear welling at the end of it.

And then something happens, after all.

2

THE ROOM VANISHES around me. The world smears sideways behind my eyelids, blurring into an infinity of colors. I figure I'm dead.

It's a pretty solid bet: Generalized Roseville Malady has a lot of symptoms and side effects, but the most noticeable one is sudden death. I don't want to go into all the jargon—Charm is the science nerd, bio and chem double major, headed for a prestigious internship at Pfizer—but essentially, my ribosomes are ticking time bombs. They're supposed to fold my proteins into clever little origami shapes, which they've been doing, mostly, but one day they're going to go haywire and start churning out garbage. My organs will fill up with mutant proteins, murderous fleets of malformed paper cranes, and I'll drown in my own fucked-up biological destiny.

I figure that day is today. It occurs to me what a twisted sense of humor the universe has, to kill me in the highest tower in the land just as

I pricked my finger on a spindle's end. I wonder if I look hot, sprawled limp and lifeless among the roses. I wonder if that will be the very last thing I wonder.

But my vision isn't going dark. The world is still rushing past me, colors and sounds and flashing by like riffled pages. I assume at first this is the life-flashing-before-my-eyes thing, but it seems longer and stranger than the twenty-one years I've lived.

And the faces I see don't belong to me. They belong to a thousand other girls reaching out toward a thousand spinning wheels or spindles or splinters. Other sleeping beauties, in other stories? I want to stop them, shout some kind of warning—*stop, you boneheads!*

One of them seems to hear me. She looks up at me with eyes that are an impossible shade of cerulean, her face framed by locks of literal gold, her finger hovering a centimeter above the spindle's end. Her lips frame a single word: "*Help.*"

The world stops smearing.

I am still on my feet. Still slightly drunk. Still touching a throbbing finger to something sharp. But everything else is different: the spinning wheel before me is polished smooth with use, the bobbin wound with flaxen thread, the distaff gleaming wickedly. The water-stained plywood of the floor has been replaced by smooth flagstones, the rickety windows by narrow, glassless slits. A cool wind slinks through them, smelling of midnight and magic.

I look up, reeling, and meet those ridiculous eyes again. They belong to a girl so gorgeous she veers from the beautiful toward the unnerving. Nobody outside a fashion magazine has skin without pores or lips the color of actual rose petals. Nobody outside a Ren faire wears dresses with pleats and girdles and trailing sleeves.

"Oh!" she says, and even her voice is fucking musical. "From whence have you come?"

I want to assure her that none of this is real. That she and her tower are hallucinations produced by the last desperate misfires of my synapses. That her usage of *whence* was grammatically suspect at best, anachronistic at worst.

I manage a single wheezy, "Holy *shit*," before my vision goes black.

❀ ❀ ❀

I WAKE UP in bed. Not mine; mine is a twin mattress with faded Disney sheets that I grew out of years ago but don't see the point in replacing. This bed is an absurd, canopied affair of white silk and soft down. It's the sort of bed that only exists in period romances and fairy tales, because actual medieval beds were a lot smellier and lumpier; the sort of bed where a princess might sleep comfortably for a hundred years.

I part the canopy with one finger and find a room that matches the bed: dark stone and rich rugs, tapestries and carved-oak chests. I blink into the cheery morning light for several seconds, half expecting a songbird to alight on the windowsill and break into an upbeat chorus, before sinking calmly back against the pillows.

This is the point in your standard fantasy adventure where the heroine would give herself a good hard pinch to determine whether or not she's dreaming. But I can hear the labored thump of my heart in my ears, feel the slightly hungover scratchiness of my eyeballs: I'm not sleeping. I'm not hallucinating. Unless the afterlife is even more profoundly wacky than most major religions have so far posited, I'm not dead. Which means—

I can't seem to finish the thought. It

sends a giddy, hysterical thrill up my spine and a nameless rush of something behind my ribcage.

My phone hums in my jean pocket. I fish it out to find roughly eight hundred texts from Charm. Most of them are variations of *wtf wtf* WTF *where are you* interspersed with threats upon my person (if this is some kind of sick joke I swear to jesus I will kill you before the grm does) and pleas for a response (hey your parents are calling me now and idk what to say so if you're alive NOW'S THE TIME BITCH).

I start to type back an apology then pause, wondering about data rates between Ohio and wherever the hell I am and how *exactly* I have cell signal, before that wild hysteria bubbles over. I write sorry babe. got spider-verse-ed into a fairy tale.

As I hit send, I feel that unfamiliar rushing in my chest again, and it turns out it has a name, after all. Oh, *hell.* You'd think twenty-one years under a life sentence would be enough to squash all the hope out of me, but here I am, lying in a bed that doesn't belong to me, filled with the desperate, foolish hope that maybe my story is about to change.

The phone buzzes in my palm: is this a joke to you

Followed by: i thought you were dead/abducted!!! what the HELL zin???

I'm tapping out a longer explanation when that impossible girl with the impossible hair sweeps aside the canopy and carols, "Oh, you're awake! Thank goodness!"

I squint at her—this slender golden princess limned in dawn light, her cheeks flushed and her eyes shining—and slowly raise my phone, take her picture, and send it to Charm with the caption *not joking.*

"Are you well?" the princess asks earnestly. "Should I call for a healer?"

I ignore her, choosing instead to watch Charm's

little typing bubble appear and disappear several times. It's worth mentioning at this juncture that Charm is profoundly, disastrously gay, and suffers from a diagnosable hero complex. Willowy princess-types with slender wrists and visible collarbones are essentially her kryptonite.

The bubble reappears. who is thjat

*that

I grin up at the princess, who now has two tiny lines marring her perfect brow. "What's your name?" I ask.

She tilts her chin very slightly upward. "I am Princess Primrose of Perceforest. And who are *you?*" I detect a hint of haughtiness in that *you,* as if she barely restrained herself from adding *peasant* after it.

"Zinnia Gray of, uh, Ohio." My eyes return to my phone. Princess

Mothereffing Primrose, apparently, I type. *dude, where did you get that spinning wheel??*

pam's corner closet & more. Pam's is the nearest flea market to our old high school and an extremely unlikely place to purchase an accursed or enchanted object. It's mostly just used vacuums and Beanie Babies perched on moldy piles of *National Geographics.*

"Lady Zinnia." The princess's voice is less musical when she's annoyed. "If I could but beg your attention for a moment. I would very much like to know how you came to be in the tower with me last night."

I slide the phone into my hoodie pocket and scooch upright in bed, legs crossed. "Is there coffee in this universe? No? Okay, just sit down." From Primrose's expression, I suspect she's not accustomed to being invited to sit on her own bed by sickly, short-haired interdimensional travelers in unwashed jeans. "Please," I add.

Primrose perches at the foot of the bed, her posture painfully upright.

"How about we start with you. What exactly were you doing in that tower room?" I'm seventy-five, maybe eighty percent sure I already know.

She draws a measured breath, and for the first time I catch a gleam of something raw beneath the porcelain-doll perfection of her face. "I—don't know. It was my first-and-twentieth birthday yesterday." Of course it was. "And I went to sleep very late. My dreams were strange, unsettled, full of a green light that called my name . . . And then I woke in a room I'd never seen before! Far from my bed, reaching for that strange object."

"You mean the spinning wheel?"

Her pale face grows two shades paler, and the raw thing in her eyes swims closer to the surface: a desperate, lonely terror. "I thought it must be," she breathes. "I'd never seen one 'til last evening."

"Because, I assume, your father ordered them all destroyed?" Standard Perrault stuff, repeated by the Grimms a hundred years later and canonized by Disney in the '50s.

Primrose stares at me for a long second, then nods.

"Mother says he spent months riding the countryside, holding bon-
fires in every village. He was trying to save me." I can hear the weariness in her voice, the exhaustion of being unsavable. Dad used to
spend hours on the phone with specialists and experimental labs and
miserly insurance companies, mortgaging the house in his search for
a cure that doesn't exist, trying so hard to save me that he nearly lost
me. He stopped only when I begged.

"Hold on a second." I slide my phone back out and start to text
Dad, wimp out, and write Charm instead. can you tell mom & dad I'm
not dead pls?

already done, she writes back, because she is, and I cannot stress
this enough, the best.

"Okay, continue."

The princess appears to brace herself for a grand speech. "I am
cursed, you see. Twelve fairies were invited to my christening feast. But a thirteenth fairy arrived, unin-
vited!" I don't think I've ever heard a person
speak with so many implied exclamation
points. It's exhausting. "A most wicked
creature who placed a curse upon
me—"

"To prick your finger on your
twenty-first birthday and fall
down dead? That sound right?"

Primrose deflates slightly. "An enchanted sleep."

"Lucky you."

"You think it *lucky* to be cursed to
sleep for a century—"

"Yeah, I do." It comes out harsher than

I mean it to. I swallow hard. "I'm sorry. Look. I'm—cursed, too. Last night was my twenty-first birthday. I was in my own world, minding my own business. I pricked my finger on a spindle as a joke, and all of a sudden I was here. In an honest-to-Jesus *castle* with an honest-to-Jesus *princess*. And historically inaccurate furnishings."

The lines have reappeared between Primrose's brows. "Was it a wicked fairy that cursed you, as well?"

I consider trying to explain that my world doesn't have curses or fairies. That my fate was determined by lax environmental regulations and soulless energy executives and plain old bad luck. "Sure, yeah," I say instead. "Except I'm going to die, not sleep, and there's nothing anybody can do to save me." But hope flutters in my chest again. I'm in a land of magic and miracles now, not ribosomes and proteins. Who knows what is or isn't possible?

"I'm sorry," says the princess, and I can tell she means it. Most people don't know what to do when I tell them I'm dying. They flinch or look away or step back, as if bad luck is contagious, or they go all maudlin and grip your hands and tell you how brave you are. Primrose just looks at me, steady and sorry, like she knows exactly how much it sucks, and neither pities nor admires me for it.

I feel snot gathering in my throat and cough it away. "It's not a big deal, it's fine," I lie. I can tell that she knows it's a lie, because she's spent roughly twenty-one years telling herself the same one, but she doesn't call me on it.

"Well. Thank you, however you came to be here. I've never met anyone else . . ." *Cursed,* I think, but she says, "Like me." She gives me a furtive, hungry look that causes me to suspect the life of a cursed princess is several degrees lonelier than the life of a dying girl.

Primrose clears her throat. "And thank you for saving me from my curse. At least for now." She looks toward her bedroom door, eyes flashing eerie green. "I still feel it calling to me. I haven't slept all night for fear I will wake in that tower room, reaching toward that wheel. Perhaps if I destroy it—my father would surely burn it if he knew—"

"No!" Panic makes my voice overloud. "I mean, please don't. I'm pretty sure that thing is my only ticket out of here. It must be a portal or something, a match to the one back home." A sly little voice whispers *are you sure you want to go home?* I elect to ignore it.

Primrose looks doubtful. "But what if it sends you into an enchanted sleep, as it would me?"

"Maybe. I don't know the rules, man." I run my fingers through the greasy tangle of my hair. "I'm just saying don't set it on fire yet. Give me a second to think."

Primrose opens her mouth to respond, but a light tap comes at the door. A voice calls, "Your Majesty. Your father requests your presence in the throne room."

I watch the pale bob of her throat as the princess swallows. "Of course. A moment, only." She spins back to me. "I have to go. Stay hidden until my return." It's an order, casually issued, as if she can't imagine anyone disobeying her.

I bow my head as she sweeps from the room.

I scroll through the ten or fifteen messages I've missed from Charm (are you okay tho? are there pharmacies in fairyland??) and type back: I only have 35% battery so I'm turning this off in case of emergencies. xoxo ummmm this IS an emergency. why are you not freaking out. why are you not trying to come back.

I start to type because but can't decide what comes next. Because I don't want to, at least not yet. Because I've fallen out of my own story and into one that might have a happy ending. Because this is my last chance to have a real adventure, to escape, to do more than play out the clock.

In the end I just write i'll come back. cross my heart, before turning my phone off. Then I wallow my way out of Primrose's ridiculous bed, steal a gown from her wardrobe, and slip out the door after her.

3

WHEN I WAS eleven, I used my Make-a-Wish
Foundation wish to spend a night in the
Disney castle and get the full princess experience. It was a total letdown. I think I
waited too long: eleven is old enough to
see the cracks in the plaster, to sense the
pity behind the megawatt smiles of the staff.
It was like trying to play with my Barbies a year
after I'd outgrown them, perfectly remembering
how it used to feel but unable to feel it again.

Primrose's castle is about a thousand times better. The stone is smooth and cool beneath my tennis
shoes and the torch brackets smell of oil and char.
My dress isn't polyester and plastic; it hangs heavy
on my shoulders, literal pounds of burgundy velvet
and gold thread. I try to walk like Primrose, a glide
so delicate it suggests my feet touch the earth only
by happenstance.

I pass a pair of women who I think might be actual chambermaids and they pause to stare, mouths

slightly open. Maybe it's my haircut or my shoes, or the fact that I couldn't figure out the laces and strings in the back of the dress and left it gaping open like one of those terrible paper hospital gowns. Whatever. Surely they're used to inbred nobility with eccentric habits of dress.

I wave cheerily at them and they fall into belated curtsies. "Which way to the throne room?"

One of the maids points wordlessly down the hall. I attempt a regal nod in return, which causes one of them to giggle and the other to elbow her.

The throne room looks exactly like you might expect a throne room to look: a long hall with vaulted ceilings and high windows. There are honest-to-God *knights* stationed along the walls, surrounding a small crowd of people who look like lost extras from the set of *A Knight's Tale*, all puffed sleeves and sweeping trains. A ruby-red carpet splits the room, leading to a man and woman sitting on golden chairs.

Primrose looks nothing like her parents. I guess when twelve fairies bless you with hotness, you lose some of the family quirks. The Queen has ordinary brown hair, a too-long nose, and an expression of permanent weariness; the King is roundish and baldish and alcoholic-looking. Standing beside them, Primrose looks like one of those Renaissance angels descended among mortals, softly glowing. I touch my own chin—the tiny, too-sharp chin I got straight from Mom—and almost like it for the first time in my life.

Primrose's eyes flick up at my movement. They widen very slightly. I give her a cheery shrug.

Before she can either banish me or die of embarrassment, the King taps his ringed knuckle against the arm of his throne. The court falls quiet. "It is my very great pleasure to announce that the curse laid upon our fair princess has failed! She is one-and-twenty years old, and yet untouched by that wicked promise!" His accent is vaguely English, the way medieval accents are in movies, and his voice booms exactly like a king's should. When the clapping and hurrah-ing dies down, he continues, "And it is my even greater pleasure to announce my daughter's betrothal!" I guess exclamation points are inheritable. "To none other than the good Prince Harold of Glennwald!"

It's only then that I notice the person standing on the other side of the thrones: a twenty-something man wearing a tunic and an expression of criminal smugness. He's handsome, in that generic, Captain America–ish way that does absolutely nothing for me, and I can tell from the briefest glance at Primrose that I'm not alone. She's smiling, but there's a falseness to it that reminds me of those Disneyland actresses when I was eleven.

That smile jars me, like a little shock of static or a missed step on the stairs. I know this story really, really well: after the curse is broken, Prince Charming marries the princess and they live happily ever after, the end. But this version has slid sideways somehow, like a listing ship. The curse isn't quite broken, the prince isn't quite charming, and that's not a happily ever after I see swimming in the princess's eyes.

The King has been speechifying for some time about his hopes for their blessed union and Prince Harold's many virtues. "—a true son to us, who has tirelessly striven to end the curse for years now, even tracking the fairy to her lair, though she fled before his might." I squint at Harold, all jawline and puffed pride; surely even an off-brand discount-store Maleficent could take him if she wanted to. "That their marriage may be delayed no longer, Princess Primrose and her betrothed will speak their vows in three days hence!"

There's a final swell of applause as Primrose and Harold step before the thrones and clasp hands. Primrose's hand looks limp and boneless in his, like a small, skinned animal.

I lurk at the back of the crowd for a while after that, smiling and nodding and collecting odd looks, before a voice hisses, "What do you think you are *doing*?"

I spin to face Primrose and sweep her my most absurd curtsy. "Why, Your Majesty, may I not celebrate your engagement?" Oh God, now I'm doing the fake British accent thing.

She barely seems to hear me, her face still gritted in that plastic smile, her pupils wide and hunted. "Your hair, your shoes . . . you look *deranged*. If anyone sees you—my father's court does not take kindly to the uncanny!"

Her hand clamps around my bicep and steers me into a side hall. "Return to my rooms and wait for me." I cross my arms and give her my best *make me* glare. "Please," she adds, looking at me with those enormous eyes of hers, "I beg of you."

I'm at least three-quarters straight, but her lashes are very long and very golden and I'm not made of stone. I nod. She closes her eyes as if summoning some inner strength before swishing back into the throne room with her smile shining like a shield.

I get lost two or three times on the way back up,

startling a pair of amorous knights in a broom closet and briefly alarming a cook. By the time I climb all nine hundred stairs I can hear my pulse a little too loudly in my own ears, feel my lungs pressing too hard against my ribs. I think of my morning handful of pills back in Ohio and the last round of X-rays that showed the chambers of my heart shrinking, my lungs congested. I hadn't showed them to Charm.

Primrose's room is warm and sunshiny and quiet. I shrug out of the burgundy velvet gown and curl in her window in my socks and hoodie, staring out at the countryside like a girl in a Mucha ad, thinking about curses and fairies and stories gone sideways. Thinking that I should probably go find that magic spindle and prick my finger and peace out of this entire medieval hallucination.

Instead, I wait. I watch the slow creep of shadows and the lazy dance of dust motes in the air. The sun is squatting fat and red on the horizon by the time Primrose returns.

She's still stunning, but I must be getting used to it, because I can see past the shine to the weary set of her mouth, the grim line of her spine. She sets a silver platter of heaped food on the seat beside me and collapses back onto her bed, vanishing behind the canopy with a dramatic sigh.

I take three enormous bites of something that I recognize from the Great British Bake-Off as a hand-raised pie. "So." I swallow. "Harold seems nice."

"Yes." Her voice is muffled, as if she's facedown in a pillow.

"Good-looking, if you're into cleft chins."

"Quite."

"And yet I can't help but detect a tad of reluctance on your part."

There's a short sigh from behind the canopy. "He's—it's—fine. I'm fine." It's a lie but I let it stand because she did the same for me, and sometimes lies are lifeboats.

The sheets rustle as Primrose rolls over. "Anyway, it hardly matters. None of them understand that the curse is still . . . waiting. Calling to me. Eventually I'll have to sleep, and I fear I will wake again only as my finger pricks the spindle's end."

I struggle not to roll my eyes at this excessive drama. "Okay, but like, just let me zap myself back to Ohio and then you can set it on fire or whatever. Boom, curse dodged."

Primrose sits up slowly, brushing aside the curtains and meeting my eyes. "I searched for it, after supper," she says softly. "I could not find the spinning wheel, nor the room, nor indeed the tower. It has vanished."

I think: oh, shit. I say, "Oh, shit." The princess doesn't flinch, so either they don't have swears in Fake-ass Medieval Fairy Land or Primrose isn't as proper as she seems. "Well, at least there's Harold. If you fall into an enchanted sleep, nine out of ten doctors recommend true love's kiss—"

"Harold is not my true love. I *assure* you." Her lips are thin and pale, twisted with revulsion. "I don't think—I don't know that there's any escaping it."

"No. There is, there has to be." I'm standing for some reason, my fingers curled into useless fists. I remind myself that this isn't my problem or business or story. That I should be sitting at home with my parents for whatever time I have left, like I promised I would, rather than gallivanting through the multiverse without my meds.

"Look. Both of us should have died or been cursed or whatever last night, on our twenty-first birthdays. But something messed it up. Our lines got crossed." I picture that listing ship again, or maybe a train leaping off its tracks and hurtling into the unknown. "It feels like we have a chance to make it come out different. To do something." I haven't wanted to "do something" since I was sixteen, packing my backpack and planning my escape.

The princess sighs a long, defeated sigh, but I can see a foolish flicker of hope in her eyes. "Like what?"

"Like . . ." The idea leaps from my skull fully formed, armored and Athenian and deeply stupid. I love it. "Like taking matters into our own hands." I feel a slightly demented smile stretching my face. "Where's this wicked fairy, exactly?"

4

THE THING ABOUT bad ideas is that they're contagious. I watch mine infect the princess, her expression sliding from bafflement to horror to frozen fascination.

"Her lair lies through the Forbidden Moor," she says slowly. "At the peak of Mount Vordred."

"Yeah, that sounds about right. How long would it take to get there? By, uh, horse or whatever?"

"It took Prince Harold three days of swift riding."

Her answer initiates a complex series of calculations involving the number of missed pills over the amount of preexisting protein buildup, magnified by physical exertion and divided by the number of days I have left. If I were a machine, all my warning lights would be blinking. I ignore them.

"We'll need supplies and food and stuff. Do you have anything more . . . rugged to wear?"

Primrose is watching me as if I'm a grisly car accident or a public marriage proposal: gruesome but mesmerizing. "It won't work, you know."

I'm already rooting through her wardrobe, looking for something free of ruffles, lace, pleats, bows, satin, ribbons, or pearls and not finding it. I wish briefly but passionately that I'd been zapped into a different storyline, maybe one of those '90s girl power fairy tale retellings with a rebellious princess who wears trousers and hates sewing. (I know they promoted a reductive vision of women's agency that privileged traditionally male-coded forms of power, but let's not pretend girls with swords don't get shit done.)

Primrose tries again. "She is powerful and cruel, and terribly ancient. Some say she has lived seven mortal lives!" I try not to let my pulse leap or my hands shake, to remind myself that hope is for suckers. "She evaded my father's men for one-and-twenty years. Even when Prince Harold—"

"Harold does not strike me as a Perceforest's best and brightest."

"But neither are we, surely!"

I spin to face her, arms full of satin ruffles. "So what's your plan? Stay here and wait for the curse to catch you, like you did for the first twenty-one years of your life? Close your eyes and go to sleep and let the world go on without you?" My voice is an angry hiss, but I don't know which of us I'm angry at.

Primrose's face is a waxy green color, her lips pressed white. I step closer. "In my world there's nothing I can do to save myself. No curse to break, no fairy to defeat. But it's different here. You can do something other than stand around and wait." I riffle through my mental box of inspirational quotes and come up with a Dylan Thomas line that I actually know from *Interstellar*. "Do not go gentle into that good night, princess. I beg of you."

She must be susceptible to begging too, because she stares at me for another breathless second before inclining her head infinitesimally. "All right."

I clap my palms together. "Swell. Now do you happen to have a magic sword or anything? An enchanted amulet? A shield imbued with special powers?"

I'm mostly joking, but Primrose wrings her hands, thumbs rubbing hard along slender wrists. "Well." She kneels and reaches beneath the soft down of her mattress, emerging with something that gleams cruelly in the reddening dusk. "There's this."

It's a long, narrow knife, sharp as glass and black as sin. It looks out of place among the feather pillows and ball gowns of Primrose's world, as if it belongs to some other, darker story. "Where the *hell* did you get that?"

Primrose holds the knife flat on her palms. "A traveling magician sold it to me when I was sixteen. He swore to me that a single cut was enough to end a life." She says it flatly, matter-of-factly, but her eyes have gone hollow and her face is waxy again and suddenly I don't feel jokey at all. Suddenly I wonder why a princess would sleep with a poison blade beneath her bed, why she would purchase it in the first place.

I picture myself at sixteen, a scarecrow of a girl stuffed with hormones and hunger instead of straw, so sick of dying I would do anything to live. I ran very different calculations in those days, comparing the Greyhound bus schedule to the number of hours before my parents would report me missing, multiplying hoarded pills by the number of days I would have on the run. I figured I could make it to Chicago before the cops were even looking for me, and from there I could go—anywhere. Do anything. Steal a few months or years for myself rather than feeding them all to my parents and their broken hearts.

Except I told Charm before I ran, and she instantly told Dad. He came up to my room looking like—I try not to remember it, actually. His face was a snapshot of my own death, a time-lapse video of the devastation I would leave behind me. We made a deal that night: if I promised not to run away, he promised to stop trying so hard to keep me.

A week later I took the SAT and dropped out of high school with my parents' blessing. Dad paid my application fee and I enrolled at Ohio University that fall. I loved it. The food was bad and my roommate was a nightmare who kept trying to sell me essential oils, but it was the first time I'd felt like a real adult. Like someone who owned their future, who belonged to no one but herself.

That feeling had been trickling away all summer as I folded myself back into the teenage-shaped hole I left behind at my parents, but what would I have done without that brief escape? What if I'd been trapped with no future and no friends, like Primrose? Perhaps I would have turned toward a darker, uglier kind of escape.

I take the knife from Primrose very, very carefully. "How . . . helpful. I'll carry this, okay?" I wrap it in the least expensive-looking skirt I can find. "So. Which way to the stables?"

"What—you mean now? *Tonight?*"

Apparently Primrose never learned dying girl rule #1: *move fast.* "Yes, dummy. How long do you think you can go without sleep?"

❈ ❈ ❈

IN THE FOLLOWING hour, several things become clear to me.

First, that Primrose isn't quite as helpless and damsel-in-distress-ish as I thought. Rather than sneaking through the castle and making off with a pair of horses by moonlight, she simply informs the stable hands that she and her ladies are going for a dawn ride through the countryside and would like two horses saddled and waiting with a picnic packed for six, please and thank you. "They won't miss us for hours, this way," she says calmly.

Second, that I do not technically "know" how to ride a "horse," to quote an unnecessarily shocked princess. "But how do you travel in your land? Surely you do not walk?" I consider explaining about internal combustion engines and state highways and asking if she'd like to try driving a stick shift with a sketchy second gear. I shrug instead.

Third, that one cannot learn to ride a horse in five minutes, at least not well enough to be trusted on a midnight journey to the Forbidden Moor.

I wind up perched behind the princess on a pile of folded blankets, clinging desperately to her traveling cloak and thinking that Charm would give a year of her life to be cozied up behind Primrose as she galloped into the night on a daring half-cocked rescue mission.

Even I can admit it's pretty cool. The air is clean and sharp and the stars reel above us like ciphers or hieroglyphs, stories written in a language I don't know. The trees are dark Arthur Rackham-ish tangles on either side of the road, reaching for us with wicked fingers while the night birds sing strange songs. My lungs ache and my legs are numb and I know Dad would have a stroke if he could see me, but he can't, and for tonight at least my life is my own, to waste or squander or give to someone else, no matter how little of it might be left.

We stop twice that night. The first time in a grove of tall pines, silver-blue in the moonlight, where the horse's hooves are silenced by soft needles. I don't so much dismount as fall sideways, barely managing to keep my phone uncrushed in my back pocket. The princess makes a graceful, sweeping gesture that somehow ends with her standing beside her horse, cloak pooled elegantly around her slippered feet. Her shoulders are a bowed line.

I don't generally do a lot of worrying about other people, except for Charm and my parents, but even I can see she's tired. "We could sleep here if you like." I poke the deep-piled pine needles. "It's nice and squashy."

Primrose shakes her head. "I'd like to be further from the castle before I sleep." There's a green gleam in her eyes as she looks back the way we came.

We ride on.

The next time we stop is beneath a gnarled hawthorn, where the earth is bare and knotted with roots. Primrose's dismount looks much more like mine this time, her legs stiff, her hands clumsy. I half catch her in my arms, thinking only briefly how heroic I look before settling her between the least lumpy roots. By the time I tuck our extra clothes and blankets around her, she's asleep.

Which is just as well, because that way she can't comment on my intelligence or life skills as I wrangle the saddle off the horse and loop her reins around a low branch. The princess's horse must be a patient soul, because she merely gives me a long-suffering ear flick rather than stomping me into jelly.

I pull my arms inside my hoodie sleeves and hunch against the warm leather of the saddle, looking up at stars through the crosshatched branches and doubting very much that I'll be able to sleep.

I must be wrong, because I wake abruptly, my legs stiff and damp, dew-soaked. The sky is the profound, reproachful black of four in the morning and someone is moving nearby.

It's Primrose, standing, her head tilted oddly to one side, her eyes wide open. There's a sickly shine to them, like the reflection of something poisonous.

"Princess?" She doesn't seem to hear me. She takes a step deeper into the woods, then another, as if there's an invisible thread tugging her deeper into a labyrinth. "Primrose!"

I heave upright and stumble toward her, grabbing her shoulders and shaking hard. "Jesus, *wake up!*" She does. I feel the weird tension slide out of her body, her arms un-tensing beneath my hands. I release her.

"Lady Zinnia?" She looks back at me with eyes that are vague and sleep-soft, perfectly blue once more. "What—oh. Dear."

I swallow the stale taste of fear. "Yeah." It's one thing to read about dark enchantments and fairy curses; it's quite another to watch them take hold of a woman's will and march her like a porcelain puppet toward her own doom. The Disneyland sheen of this place is wearing thin, like paint peeling to reveal black mold running beneath it.

I shrug at her with my hands shoved deep in my jean pockets. "I'll keep watch, if you want to get a little more sleep."

She worries at her lower lip with teeth that are too white in the dark. She nods and curls back among the hawthorn roots, arms wrapped tight around herself, hair spilling over her cloak.

I watch in silence until her body uncoils and her fingers unclench. Afterward I find myself squinting into the spaces between trees, looking for a hint of green or the shine of a spindle's end, getting steadily more spooked by the cool touch of wind down my neck and the soft scuttling sounds of night creatures in the woods. I decide it's a good time to check my phone.

There are several dozen more texts from Charm, mostly threats upon my person should I fail to return; a handful from Dad, their tone genial listing toward worried; one from the Roseville Public Library informing me that I now owe them $15.75 in fines and/or my firstborn child.

A few hours ago it had seemed like a perfectly fine idea to go have a little adventure, face down a fairy, rescue a princess (and maybe, somehow, myself), and zap back home like Bilbo strolling back into the Shire. But now—huddled in the cold dark with a cursed princess and a tightness in my chest that's either terror or impending death—I'm feeling more like Frodo, whose story was full of danger. Who never did get to return home, or at least not for long.

I text Charm. going to face Maleficent and break curse, should be home in three days.

She texts back so fast I feel a hot stab of guilt, knowing she's sleeping with her ringer on. how are you getting home??

portkey?

there's no such thing as portkeys asshole. A brief pause. and i thought
we agreed never to mention joanne or her works ever again

I consider asking her how she would explain interdimensional
travel into overlapping fictional narratives, but Charm probably has
at least three solid theories she would like to discuss. At length. With
slides. So instead I lean over to take another picture of Primrose. Even
on my mediocre camera, blurred and dim, she's luminous. Her face
glows white out of the gloom, a sleeping beauty by way of Rembrandt.

A slight pause before she replies: do not attempt to distract me with
your hot imaginary friend. I repeat: there's no such thing as portkeys

says who

says physics

hon, I respond patiently, I am currently on a quest to find and defeat a
wicked fairy. pretty sure the laws of physics no longer apply

the laws of physics always apply, that's why we call them laws

There's a long gap while her texting bubble appears and disappears.
give her hell from me, babe

I can almost hear the rasp of Charm's voice as she says it, the sudden sincerity that no one expects from a girl with a giant Golden Age
Superman tattoo on her shoulder. There's no reason to choke up over
it, so I don't. I send her another *xoxo* and power the phone off before
the battery can dip below 20 percent.

After that I sit with my arms around my shins and my cheek on my
knees, watching the dawn paint the princess in silver and shadow and
wondering what it would feel like to sleep and keep sleeping. Better
than dying, I guess, but Jesus—what a shitty story the two of us were
given. I don't know about the moral arc of the universe, but our arcs
sure as hell don't bend toward justice.

Unless we change them. Unless we grab our narratives by the ear

and drag them kicking and screaming toward better endings. Maybe the universe doesn't naturally bend toward justice either; maybe it's only the weight of hands and hearts pulling it true, inch by stubborn inch.

❀ ❀ ❀

"So, why is the moor forbidden?" I'm aiming for nonchalant, but my voice sounds tense in my ears. "Are there flying monkeys? Rodents of Unusual Size?"

"What?"

"Just checking."

It's the morning of the third day and we've abandoned the road, picking our way over scrubby hills and wind-scoured stone. The sun is grayish and reluctant here, as if it's shining through greasy paper, and the trees are stunted and crabbed.

Primrose has pulled the horse to a stop before a pair of tall, jagged stones. They aren't carved with strange symbols or glowing or anything, but there's something deliberate about the angle of them, like they aren't there by accident.

The princess makes her graceful dismount and touches her palm to the sharp edge of the stone. "It's forbidden because my father wishes to protect his people, and the moor is dangerous if you don't know the way."

"Do we know the way?"

"Harold told me. In some detail." The flatness of her tone suggests that Harold is one of those men whose conversations are more like long, boastful speeches. "I listened well."

Without the slightest change of expression, without even drawing a breath, Primrose drags her palm hard across the edge. When she draws back the stone shines slick and dark with blood.

"*Jesus*, Primrose, what are you doing?"

She doesn't answer, but merely lifts her hand to the sky, palm up. I watch her blood run down her wrist, red as roses, red as riding hoods. I was so sure I'd landed in one of those soft, G-rated fairy tales, stripped of medieval horrors; I can feel it shifting beneath my feet, twisting toward the kind of tale where prices are paid and blood is spilled.

A shape wings toward us across the moor, ragged and black. It lands on the standing stone in a rush of feathers, and for the first time in my life I fully appreciate the difference between a crow and a raven. This bird is huge and wild-looking, clearly built for midnights dreary rather than McDonald's parking lots.

It dips forward and laps at Primrose's palm with a thick tongue and this, I find, is a little much. "Okay, what the *fuck?*"

"We'll leave Buttercup behind and continue on foot," Primrose says evenly. "Walk close behind me, and do not stray to either side." The raven launches back into the air, cutting a curving path through the smeary sky, and lands on a low branch a quarter mile ahead. Primrose follows it, stepping between the standing stones with her bloodied palm held tight to her chest. I follow them both, muttering about antibiotics and blood poisoning and tetanus, feeling the cold knock of the knife against my ribs, hoping to God all this nonsense is worth it.

❖   ❖   ❖

BY NIGHTFALL, A mist has risen. I'm tired and hungry and my muscles are shuddering from three days without supplements or steroids.

Primrose isn't much better; the curse has woken her at midnight for each of the last three nights, the pull growing stronger each time. I'm not sure she slept at all last night, but merely curled beneath her cloak with her eyes screwed shut, fighting the silent call of her spell.

The damn bird leads us in circles and loops, twisting and doubling back so many times I come very close to stomping off on a path of my own making, screw magic—but the shadows fall strangely across the moor. I keep thinking I see dark shapes creeping beside us, furred and clawed, gone as soon as I turn to look.

I stay behind Primrose. We keep following the raven.

I don't know if it's the mist or something more, but the mountains arrive all at once: black teeth erupting before us, crooked and sharp. A rough road coils up from the moor, biting into the mountainside and ending in a structure so ruinously Gothic, so bleak and desperate, it can only belong to one person in this story.

"Should we approach by the main road?" Primrose whispers. "Or go around, perhaps sneak in and take her by surprise?"

At some point I suppose I should stop being surprised when the princess is more than a doe-eyed maiden, ready to faint prettily at the first sign of danger. I'm always annoyed when people are surprised that I have a personality beyond my disease, as if they expect me to be nothing but brave smiles and blood-spotted handkerchiefs.

I watch the raven spiral up the mountain. It soars through a narrow slit at the top of the tallest tower of the castle. "Oh, I think we can probably just knock on the front door, like civilized folk." Even before I finish speaking the window pulses with a faint, greenish light. "She already knows we're coming."

5

The path up the mountain doesn't take as long as it ought to. We've barely rounded the first turn in the road when we find ourselves standing at the foot of the castle. Up close it's even more unsettling: the battlements jagged and uneven, the stones stained, the windows staring like a thousand lidless eyes. All its angles seem subtly wrong, off-putting in no way I can name. I want to laugh at it; I want to run from it. I mentally compose a text to Charm instead: it's Magic Kingdom for goths. Gormenghast by Escher.

I swallow hard. My fist is raised to knock at the doors—which are exactly as tall and ornate and ghastly as you're imagining—when they swing silently inward. There's nothing but formless dark beyond them.

"Well." I glance sideways at Primrose. She's pale but unflinching, jaw tight. "Shall we?"

She nods once, her chin high, and offers me her arm. It's only once I take it that I feel her trembling.

We're barely a half step inside when a voice cracks from the walls, shrieking like bats from the eaves, everywhere at once. "Who dares enter here?"

I open my mouth to answer but Primrose beats me to it, stepping forward with her chest thrown out and her voice pitched loud, and for the first time it occurs to me that princesses grow up to be queens. "It is I, Princess Primrose of Perceforest, and the Lady Zinnia of Ohio." She turns back to me and hisses low, "Draw out the blade. Ready yourself. I will distract her."

It's a good plan. It might even work.

Except I didn't come here to kill a fairy, because I'm not a prince or a knight or a hero. I'm not Charm, who would charge a dozen dragons for me if only she knew where they lived. I'm just a dying girl, and the last rule for dying girls, the one we never say out loud, is *try not to die*.

I slide the knife from my hoodie and unwind the soft satin. I hold it aloft, showing it clearly to our unseen enemy, then toss it casually to the ground. It throws sparks as it slides across the flagstones.

"Lady Zinnia! What are you—"

I ignore Primrose. "Excuse me?" I call into the shadows. "Miss Maleficent?"

There is a long, frigid silence. Green light flares at the end of the hall, a sickly torch held in a hard-knuckled hand. The light falls across a slender wrist, a black hood, a dramatic sweep of robes. I'm distantly disappointed that she isn't wearing a horned cowl.

"That is not my name." This time the voice comes only from the black hood, a low growl instead of a shriek.

"My bad." I raise both hands, empty of weapons. "I was hoping you had a second to chat." I wait. "I will take your frozen silence for a yes.

We come to beg a favor from you." There's an indrawn breath beside me, then Primrose's voice repeating the word *beg* as if it's foreign and rather filthy.

"You want the enchantment lifted, I suppose." I don't know if I'm imagining the bitter irony in the fairy's voice.

I clear my throat. "Two curses, actually. You're familiar with Primrose's situation, I think, but not mine. I was . . . similarly cursed, in a land far from here. I come to you now in the hope that you—in all your infinite wisdom and limitless power, who have unlocked the secrets of life eternal"—I am aware that I'm laying it on thick and don't care, dignity is for people with more time than me—"might free us both from our misfortunes. I have no jewels or treasures to offer you, save one." I practiced this speech for the past two nights while I kept watch over the sleeping Primrose. I lift my face to that green torch light and pull my features into an expression of deepest sacrifice. "My firstborn child."

Primrose gasps again. "Zinnia, you cannot! I forbid it!"

"Chill," I tell her through slightly gritted teeth. I don't feel like explaining to her that (a) multiple doctors have informed me that my ovaries are toast and (b) I do not want and have never wanted kids, having spent my life trying to save my parents from the trolley problem of my death. Hard pass.

The hooded figure at the end of the hall takes a step, another, and then somehow she's standing directly before us, a raven perched on her shoulder and her eyes gleaming like poison through the shadows. Her gaze falls first on Primrose. "Even if I could break the spell I laid on you one-and-twenty years ago, I would not." The princess stares back, her face gone hard and cold, stark-shadowed in the torchlight.

I'm not sure I would turn my back to anyone who looked at me like that, but the fairy doesn't seem to give it much thought. "And you . . ." She takes a step toward me and snatches my hand, snake-fast. I recoil, but she holds it firm, flipping it palm up to inspect the pattern of lines and veins. She mutters as she looks, tracing a yellowed nail along one or two of the routes as if my palm is a poorly labeled map.

"Mm." She releases my hand more slowly, almost gently. Her voice, when she speaks, is even rougher. "Keep your unborn child."

"But—"

"I can't save you, girl." Her voice is a slap, harsh and hard, but there's a note of mourning behind it.

"Oh." I rub my palm hard with my thumb, blink against the nothing-at-all stinging my eyes. "Okay." I was prepared for this, really I was. Sick kids learn to calibrate their expectations early, to negotiate with their shitty luck again and again. "Okay. How about a trade? I'm basically a princess back in Ohio. Let me take Primrose's place. I'll prick my finger and fall into your enchanted sleep, and she goes free." Maybe I'll zap back into my own world stuck in some magical cryogenic stasis; maybe a handsome prince will wake me and I'll be cured. Either way, sleeping has to be better than straight-up dying. Strangers tend to imagine that sick people are looking for ways to die with dignity, but mostly we're looking for ways to live.

The fairy's eyes flash beneath her hood. "You think to save yourself."

"And her." I nod at Primrose. "I'm not a monster."

The hood shakes back and forth. "The enchantment cannot be shared or stolen or tricked. You cannot take her place." She gestures at Primrose with her torch. "She has evaded my terms, but only briefly. There is no escaping fate."

There's a sudden movement behind the fairy. I see rose lips snarling, white knuckles around a black blade. The torch clangs to the castle floor and the fairy's head is hauled back, a knife hovering a hairsbreadth above her throat. "Oh, no, fairy?" Primrose pants into her ear. The princess's eyes are green in the torchlight, burning with twenty-one years of bitter rage.

I can see the fairy's face clearly for the first time. I don't know what I was expecting—glamorous eyeliner and devastating cheekbones, perhaps, or a gnarled crone with snaggled teeth—but she's just a woman. Silvery blond, plainish and oldish and weary.

"Kill me if you like, child. It won't save you." That mournful sound has returned to her voice and her eyes are welling with some deep, grim sympathy. Shouldn't she be cackling and cursing? Shouldn't the pair of us be turned into toads or ravens? I feel the story stumbling again, another wrong note in a song I know well.

"I'm sorry." The fairy whispers it, and I think dizzily that she means it.

Primrose makes a strangled, raging, weeping sound in her throat. The knifepoint trembles. "*Sorry?* You who ruined my life and stole my future? Who cursed me?"

"I did not curse you, girl." The fairy sighs the words, long and tired, and Primrose can't seem to speak through her fury.

The fairy reaches two fingers up to the blade at her throat and suddenly it's not a blade at all but merely a feather, glossy and black. It falls from Primrose's fingers. Her eyes follow it—the feather that was once her only weapon, her way out, secret and cruel—as it slips silently, harmlessly, to the floor.

The fairy turns to face the princess. She touches the perfect arch of her cheekbone, very gently. "I *blessed* you."

❖ ❖ ❖

PRIMROSE HAS AN expression on her face that I recognize vaguely from middle school plays, when one kid said the wrong line and the other was left in baffled, sweaty limbo.

"What?" Primrose asks, with admirable calm.

"It was meant to be a blessing. It still is, by my reckoning."

A flicker of that bitter fury returns to the princess's face. "How is a century of sleep a blessing, exactly?"

"There are worse things than sleep," the fairy answers softly, and she may be the villain, but she's not wrong. "Stay a moment, and I will explain. Would you like some tea?"

The middle-school-play expression returns to Primrose's face, and probably mine. Both of us glance helplessly around at the hall, full of twisted black columns and bare stone. No place has ever looked less likely to provide a cup of tea.

"Oh!" The fairy taps her forehead. "Apologies. Let me just—"

She snaps her fingers twice. The walls quiver around us like a reflection in rippling water, and then—

We aren't in a castle anymore.

The three of us are standing in a smallish room with hardwood floors and deep-piled rugs. Everything is pleasantly domestic, bordering on cozy: there's a scarred kitchen table set with three teacups; neatly banked coals in a stone fireplace; shelves of clay jars and blue glass bottles bearing tidy cursive labels. The ghoulish green torchlight has been replaced by the honeyed glow of beeswax candles.

The fairy herself is no longer draped in black robes, but wearing a grease-spotted apron over a plain cotton skirt. A small, bright-eyed blackbird perches on her shoulder where the raven once stood.

For a second I think Primrose might fall into an actual swoon. I position myself to catch her, wondering distantly who's going to catch me because I'm one surprise away from a swoon myself. The wrong note I heard before has become an entirely wrong tune, dancing us toward God knows where.

"Forgive my little illusion," says the fairy. "I find a sufficiently menacing first impression discourages most visitors."

Primrose replies with a faint *oh*. I drift a little dazedly over to the nearest window. We're still on a mountainside, but it appears to be a much gentler mountain than the craggy peak that confronted us through the mist. I see the pale heads of wildflowers swaying in the moonlight, hear the green shushing of grass stalks in the breeze. The moor below looks more like a meadow now, all gentle curves and grassy knolls.

"So all that was just . . . an aesthetic?" Honestly, I admire her commitment. "The castle. The raven. The *blood sacrifice*—"

The fairy flinches at the word *blood*. "Oh!" She bustles to a shelf and returns to the table with an armful of clanking bottles and a length of plain cloth. "Sit, please."

Primrose sits, looking like an actor still waiting in vain for someone to give her a line. The fairy points to her hand, curled and crusted with dried blood, and Primrose blinks a little dreamily before laying it on the table between them. The fairy mutters and dabs at the cut—a raw line that strikes like red lightning across her palm—plasters it with honey, and wraps it in clean white cotton. She pats it twice when she's finished.

Primrose stares at her own hand on the table as if it's a sea creature or an alien, wildly out of place. "I don't understand." Her musical voice is ragged around the edges.

"I know. But I don't know where to begin." The fairy stares at the princess with eyes that are gentle and wry and very, very blue. I squint at her hair. Was it true gold once, before it was silver?

I take the third seat at the table and lean across it, hands clasped. "How about you start with your name?" I have a wild suspicion that I already know it.

The fairy chews at her lower lip—palest pink, like the fragile teacup roses Mom grows along the drive—before whispering, "Zellandine."

Oh, hell. I hear a small, pained sound leave my mouth. I glance at Primrose and know from the polite puzzlement of her face that she doesn't recognize the name. "She's one of us," I explain. But I'm lying; her story is far worse than ours.

"You know my tale, then?"

I was hoping until that moment that I was wrong, that Zellandine's story went differently in this world. But I can tell from the look in her eyes—a scarred-over grief, healed but still haunted—that it didn't.

I want to tell her I'm sorry, to take her hand and congratulate her for surviving. Instead I give her a stiff nod. For someone who's spent her entire life being comforted, I'm pretty shit at it.

"Were you cursed as well, then?" Primrose asks, reaching gamely for her familiar lines.

Zellandine stands abruptly. She pokes at the coals in the hearth and swings an iron pot low above them, her back turned to us. "Before there were curses—before there were fairies or roses or even spindles—there was just a sleeping girl."

Even with my Sleeping Beauty obsession, I didn't read Zellandine's version until the fifth week of FOLK 344—Dr. Bastille's Fairy Tales and Identity course. I guess it's such an ugly story that we prefer to leave it untold, moldering in the unswept corners of our past like something gone to rot in the back of the pantry.

"I was born with a disorder of the heart." Zellandine speaks to the steady heat of the coals. "If I overexerted myself or if I suffered a shock, I might fall into a faint from which no one could rouse me for a spell. It was no great matter when I was a child. But by the time I was older . . ."

She trails away and I look sideways at Primrose to see if she understands what's coming, hears the dark promise in that ellipsis. Apparently a princess's life is not so sheltered that she doesn't know what sorts of things might befall a woman who can't cry out, can't run. Her fingers curl around the white line of her bandage. "Surely your father protected you, or your mother."

"I was a maid in a king's castle, far beyond my family's protection." In the version we read in Dr. Bastille's class, a translation from medieval French, Zellandine is a princess who falls into an endless sleep when her finger is pierced by a splinter of flax. I wonder how many tiny variations there are of the same story, how many different beauties are sleeping in how many different worlds.

Zellandine lifts the pot from the fire with a fold of her apron and fills our teacups. I've read enough fantasy books and spy novels to know better than to drink anything offered to me by an enemy, especially if it smells sweet and inviting, like bruised lavender, but I no longer think Zellandine is our enemy. I curl my fingers around the cup and let the heat of it soak through skin and tendon, right down to the bone.

"Soon enough I caught the eye of the king's son. I was careful and quiet; I was sure never to tend his rooms when he was present. But one day he returned unexpectedly while I was shoveling the ashes from his hearth. He startled me when he spoke my name, and my heart betrayed me. The last thing I remember is the crack of my skull against the stones." Zellandine is seated again at the table but she still isn't looking at us. "When I woke, I was in a bed far grander than any I'd seen before. So wide my hands couldn't find the edges, so soft I felt I was drowning, suffocated by silk." Her nostrils flare wide, white-rimmed. "I can still smell it, if I'm not careful. Lye from the castle laundry, rose oil from his skin."

Right now you're thinking: *this isn't how the story goes.* You might not have a degree in this shit but you've seen enough Disney movies and picture books to know there's supposed to be a handsome prince and true love and a kiss, which can't be consensual because unconscious people can't consent, but at least it breaks the curse and the princess wakes up.

But in the very oldest versions of this story—before the Grimms, before Perrault—the prince does far worse than kiss her, and the princess never wakes up.

I make myself keep listening to Zellandine, unflinching. I always hate it when people flinch from me, as if my wounds are weapons.

"I did not tend the prince's hearth after that. I hoped—if I were quiet and careful enough—I might be safe. That it might be over." Zellandine's fingers spread against the softness of her own stomach. "Soon it became clear that it wasn't."

In that oldest story the still-sleeping princess gives birth nine months after the prince visits her in the tower. Her hungry child suckles at her fingertips and removes the splinter of flax, and only then does she wake from her poisoned sleep.

I felt sick the first time I read it, betrayed by a story that I loved, that *belonged* to me. I slouched into class the next day, arms crossed and hoodie pulled up, scowling while Dr. Bastille lectured about women's bodies and women's choices in premodern Europe, about history translated into mythology and passivity into power. "You are accustomed to thinking of fairy tales as make-believe." Dr. Bastille looked straight at me as she said it, her face somehow both searing and compassionate. "But they have only ever been mirrors."

I reread the story when I got home, sitting cross-legged on my rose-patterned sheets, and felt a terrible, grown-up sort of melancholy descending over me. I used to see Sleeping Beauty as my wildest, most aspirational fantasy—a dying girl who didn't die, a tragedy turned into a romance. But suddenly I saw her as my mere reflection: a girl with a shitty story. A girl whose choices were stolen from her.

Zellandine has fallen silent, staring at the table with her face folded tight. I take a sip of my flowery tea. "What happened to the baby?"

She looks up at me and her mouth twists. "There was no baby. I followed whispers and rumors and found a wisewoman in the mountains who knew the spell I needed. I chose a different story for myself, a better one." The memory of that choice softens her face, settling like sunlight across her features. "I stayed with the wisewoman, after. She taught me everything she knew, and I taught myself more.

I gathered power around myself until I could turn blades into feathers and huts into castles, could read the past in tea leaves and the future in the stars."

It shouldn't be possible to look intimidating sipping tea in a stained apron, but Zellandine's eyes are rich and knowing and her smile is full of secrets. The smile dims a little when she continues. "Some of the things I read there . . . I saw my own story played out over and over. A thousand different girls with a thousand terrible fates. I began to interfere, where and when I could." I feel a strange flick of shame as she says it; it seems that some dying girls follow different rules and dedicate themselves to saving others, rather than themselves.

"A witch, they called me, or a wicked fairy. I didn't care." Zellandine turns the rich blue of her gaze to Primrose for the first time in a long while. "I still don't, if it saves even a single girl from the future she was given."

Primrose can't seem to look away, to move. "What fate did you see for me?" Her voice is the ghost of a whisper.

The blackbird on the fairy's shoulder tilts its head to consider Primrose with one ink-drop eye. Zellandine strokes a finger down its breast. "Surely you can guess, princess."

Primrose stares at her with brittle defiance.

"Without my curse, you would be wed by now," says the fairy, ever so gently. "How well would your marriage bed suit you, do you think?"

The princess is still silent, but I watch the defiance crack and crumble around her shoulders. It leaves her face pale and exposed, and I understand from the anguished twist of her lips that it's not only Prince Harold that she objects to, but princes in general, along with knights and kings and probably even handsome farm boys.

Zellandine continues in the same gentle, devastating voice. "I saw a marriage you did not want to a husband you could not love, who would not care whether you loved him or not. I saw a slow suffocation in fine sheets, and a woman so desperate to escape her story she might end it herself."

Primrose lifts her teacup and sets it quickly back down, her hands trembling so hard that tea sloshes over the rim. I want to pat her shoulder or touch her arm, but I don't. God, I wish Charm were here; she'd have the princess weeping therapeutically into her shoulder within seconds.

"You could have—" Primrose pauses and I watch her throat bob, like she's swallowing something barbed. "You could have done something else. Warned me or protected me, stolen me away—"

"I've tried that. I've built towers for girls and kept them locked away. I've chased them into the deep woods and left seven good men to guard them. I've turned their husbands into beasts and bears, set their suitors impossible tasks. I've done it all, and sometimes it has worked. But it's difficult to disappear a princess. There tend to be wars and hunts and stories that end with witches dancing in hot iron shoes. So I did what I could. I gave you a blessing disguised as a curse, an enchantment that would prevent your engagement and marriage. I gave you one-and-twenty years to walk the earth on your own terms, unpursued by man—"

"Oh, hardly that." Primrose's voice is beyond bitter, almost savage. It occurs to me that I got it wrong, and that the knife beneath her pillow might not have been intended for her own flesh at all. I thought she was an Aurora, empty and flat as cardboard, but she was just a girl doing her best to survive in a cruel world, like the rest of us.

"—followed by a century to sleep protected by a hedge of thorns so high no man could reach you. I gave you the hope that when you wake you will be forgotten, no longer a princess but merely a woman, and freer for it. The hope that the world might grow kinder while you sleep."

Zellandine, who is neither selfish nor a coward, reaches her hand toward Primrose's. "I'm sorry if it isn't enough. It's all I could give, and there's no changing it now."

Primrose stands before the fairy's fingers can find hers, chair scraping across the floorboards, hands curled into fists. "I can't—I need—" She reels for the door and staggers out into the velveteen night before I can do more than say her name.

The door swings stupidly behind her, swaying in the breeze. I sit watching it for a while, my tea freezing and my heart aching, before Zellandine observes, "The heaviest burdens are those you bear alone."

I transfer my blank stare to her and she adds, a little less mystically and more acerbically, "Go talk to her, girl." I do as I'm told.

6

SHE'S SITTING AMONG the pale-petaled wildflowers, her arms wrapped around her knees and her eyes fixed on the eastern horizon. Her face makes me think of those eerie Renaissance paintings of Death and the Maiden, youthful beauties dancing with alabaster skeletons.

"Hey," I offer, feebly. She doesn't answer.

I sit carefully beside her and run my fingertips over the white satin flowers. When I was a girl, I used to pull daisy petals one by one and play my own macabre version of *he loves me/he loves me not*. It went *I live/I die*, and I would keep playing until I ended on an *I live*.

"I heard you speak to me, that night. When I almost touched the spindle." She sounds distant and dreamy, as if she's talking in her sleep.

I twist at a flower stem. "I called you a bonehead."

"You told me not to do it. And it was like a spark falling into my mind, catching me on fire. I asked for your help because it was the first time I thought anyone *could* help me, that I might truly have a choice. That my own will might matter." She's staring at the horizon, where the gray promise of dawn is gathering. "I'd almost begun to believe it."

My lungs feel tight and I don't know if it's the amyloidosis or the heartbreak. "Yeah. Yeah, me too." I'd half convinced myself that I'd found a loophole, a workaround, a way out of my bullshit story. I thought the two of us together might change the rules. But even in a world of magic and miracles, both of us remain damned. I clear my throat. "I'm sorry."

Primrose shakes her head, hair rippling silver in the starlight. "Don't be. These three days have been the best of my life." I think of the long days of riding and the haunted nights among the hawthorn roots, of a raven's tongue lapping at her blood, and try not to reflect too deeply on what this says about the princess's quality of life.

"So. What now?"

She lifts her shoulder in a gesture that might be called a shrug in a less graceful person. "Return to my father's castle and bid my parents farewell. Then I suppose I prick my finger on the spindle's end, the way I was always going to. Perhaps you might do the same, and return home." She doesn't sound sad or angry; she sounds like a woman resigned to her fate. This time I'm sure the tightness in my chest is coming from my heart.

Primrose stands and offers me her hand. She tries to make herself smile and doesn't quite manage it. "Maybe we'll both wake up in a better world."

The fairy packs us seedy bread and salted meat and twelve shining apples before we leave. She takes our hands in hers and rubs her thumb across the crisscrossed lines of our palms. "Come visit me, after," she tells us, which displays what my grandmother would call *a lot of damn gall,* given that she knows we're riding toward certain death/a century-long sleep.

We cross the gentle green meadow that was once the Forbidden Moor, following a blackbird that was once a raven. I look back just before we pass through the standing stones. Instead of that ruinous castle there's only a stone hut leaning into the mountainside, sunbaked and sweet and just a little lonely. As we step between the stones the hut vanishes, hidden by greasy coils of mist and miles of gloomy moor once more. The blackbird becomes a raven again, all curved talons and ragged feathers. He watches us leave with a bright black eye.

❖ ❖ ❖

THE FIRST NIGHT we take shelter on the leeward side of a low bluff and I make a very passable fire (shoutout to Mom for making me stay in Girl Scouts through third grade). I feel like I'm getting good at this whole medieval camping thing, but Primrose can't seem to sleep. She rustles and thrashes beneath her cloak for hours before sighing and sitting up. She warms her hands by the dying coals, the fairy's bandage glowing orange across her palm. "You ought to sleep, Lady Zinnia. I can't."

Her eyes are puffy and red with exhaustion. "I won't let you wander off," I tell her. "Just so you know."

She doesn't look at me when she answers. "The curse is getting stronger. I think it's been denied long enough, and now it wants me very badly, and I must fight it all the time. I don't know if you'd be able to stop me." I can't tell if her eyes are green or blue in the dimness. Her voice gets smaller. "I wanted to see my mother once more, before the end."

We don't stop much after that. Primrose sleeps only in stolen snatches and wakes with haunted eyes. Her face goes hollow and grayish, her skin stretched like wet paper over the hard bones of her cheeks. By the third day I'm not so much clinging to her as I am holding her desperately upright.

Her head lolls forward, her hands slack on the reins.

"Hey, princess. I was wondering—who inherits the throne once you fall asleep?" I absolutely do not care about the inheritance laws of a fairy tale kingdom I'm about to zap myself out of, but I figure it's the kind of thing a princess might care about.

Her head jerks upright. "What? Oh. I believe the crown will pass to my Uncle Charles, as I have no brothers or sisters." I wonder exactly when the exclamation points left her sentences, and wish absurdly that I could restore them.

"I don't have any siblings either," I offer, sounding like an extremely boring first date. "I always wanted a little sister, but . . ." Mom and Dad said they only ever wanted one kid, but I'm pretty sure they're lying. I think they wanted to spare me from a younger sibling who would inevitably outgrow me, a 2.0 version of myself with all the bugs and fatalities worked out, but honestly I wish they'd had a second kid to pour their hearts into. "Anyway. At least I had Charm."

"Charm?" Primrose says it like a noun rather than a name.

"Haven't I mentioned her? Here." I fish my phone from my hoodie and power it on (18%). I curve my arm around the princess so she can see my lock screen: Charm simultaneously blowing me a kiss and flipping me off. It's summer and she's wearing a black tank top to show off what she refers to as her "lady-killers" (biceps) and her "job-killers" (tattoos).

Primrose looks at Charm's face for a length of time that confirms my suspicions about her. She straightens in the saddle, shutting her mouth with an almost audible click of teeth. "A friend of yours?"

"The very best." The only, really. "We met in second grade when she decked a kid for asking if my parents let me pick out my own casket. She got sent to the principal's office and I played sick so I could go sit with her in the hall. She's stuck with me ever since, despite my . . . curse." Or, if I'm being honest with myself, *because* of it.

Charm's parents already had three kids when they saw a '90s *Frontline* special about homeless youth in Russia. They "rescued" Charm from a St. Petersburg orphanage six months later and never let her forget it. Every time she misbehaved they told her to be grateful she wasn't begging on the streets; every Christmas her dad jokes that they already got her the American Dream, so what else could she want?

It gave Charm a gigantic chip on her shoulder, biweekly counseling sessions at school, and a lifelong desire to be a hero. To be the one doing the saving, rather than being saved. There's a reason she has a tattoo on her shoulder of an adopted foreign baby who grew up to save the world again and again.

I figure the GRM made me the ultimate challenge, an unrescuable damsel. Charm used to spend hours and hours with her brother's chemistry set and a stack of *Encyclopedia Britannicas*—as if a third grader was going to discover the cure to an incurable genetic disorder—until she grew out of it and gave up. At least it wasn't a complete waste of time: she blew the top off the science section of the ACT and got her pick of internships at fancy biotech companies when she graduated. (I was pushing for this tiny start-up that was trying to clone organs on the cheap, but she went with Pfizer, an objectively terrible pharmaceutical giant, for reasons I genuinely cannot fathom).

She's texted me twenty or thirty times since I last checked my phone: theories and questions and ultimatums; secondhand worries from my folks who are apparently growing concerned that my "sleepover" is now six days long; a bunch of screenshots from sites about physics and the multiverse and the infinity of alternate realities that lie one atop the other, like pages in a book.

I think about replying but can't think of anything to say. I power the phone off before I can do anything embarrassing, like cry.

"Perhaps when you return to your world, you and Charm might find your fairy and defeat her together," Primrose says. "I—I could not have faced Zellandine without you."

I shrug against her back, feeling a little guilty. I hadn't gone for her sake, after all. "Didn't do much good."

"No. Although . . ." Primrose's weary shoulders straighten a little. "Although I feel stronger than I did before, knowing the truth. It's the difference between being dragged to the gallows blindfolded and walking with your head held high and eyes wide open. It's the lesser of two evils, I suppose."

God, that's bleak. She deserves so much more than the gallows, more than this tight-laced world of towers and thorns and lesser evils. I remind myself how much I dislike being cried over and try very hard not to cry over Primrose.

"Perhaps your curse will prove more negotiable than mine. Perhaps—"

"It's not . . ." I didn't really plan on explaining teratogenic damage to a medieval princess whose medical knowledge probably involves bloodletting and wandering uteri, but it's still half a day's ride to the castle and I can't stand the note of stubborn hope in her voice. "It's not a curse, exactly, and there's no wicked fairy."

We ride, and I talk. I talk about natural gas extraction and MAL-09, the chemical compound that contaminated the tap water in Roseville

in the late '90s, which had been tested and approved on adult men—
but not pregnant women. I talk about placental barriers and genetic
damage and the forty-six infants who were born with fucked-up ribosomes in the greater Roseville area. I talk about the years and years
of legal battles, the fines that didn't matter and the settlement that
put me through college. I'm sure at least three-quarters of it is soaring
straight over Primrose's head, but she listens with an intensity that I
find weirdly flattering. In my world, everybody already knows about
Generalized Roseville Malady. They've seen the five-episode docu-
mentary on Netflix and argued with conspiracy theorists on Facebook
and to them I'm just another headline, not a story in my own right.

"Some of the other GRM kids formed a group—Roseville's
Children—that's done a lot of activism stuff. They marched on the
state capitol, did some sit-ins in Washington. They always get a lot of
press, but nothing ever seems to change. Mom and Dad took me to
the monthly meetings when I was a kid, but . . ." I trail away. I stopped
going to the Roseville's Children meetings at sixteen, when I decided I
didn't want to spend my remaining years chanting slogans and wearing
cheesy T-shirts. Now I feel another squirm of guilt, thinking of all the
sleeping beauties I hadn't even tried to save. There are fewer of us than
there used to be.

"Anyway. I'm on a ton of steroids and meds to try to delay the
protein buildup, but my last X-rays weren't great. The phrase 'weeks,
not months' was used." I aim for a casual tone, but I hear Primrose's
gasp of horror.

"I'm sorry," she says eventually, and there isn't really anything else
to say.

We ride on—we dying girls, we sorry girls, gallows-bound—until
the fairy tale spires of Perceforest Castle rise through the trees, gilded
by the setting sun.

✦ ✦ ✦

THE GROOM NEARLY faints when we turn up in the stables, smelly and tired and road-grimed. There follows a long period of shouting and running about, while the groom fetches a better-dressed groom who fetches an even better-dressed fellow, who sweeps the pair of us into the castle and up to the King's council room.

The atmosphere reminds me of a hospital waiting room, cold and airless, thick with worry. The King and Queen are seated across from Prince Harold, muttering over a map of the kingdom. They fall silent at the sight of the princess.

There follows a medieval version of the classic "young lady, where have you been, we were worried sick" speech. There are a few more "whences" and "wherefores," but it covers the same territory. I do my best to melt into a tapestry while the King thunders and the Prince tries not to look disappointed that he doesn't get to ride out in daring rescue of anyone and the Queen stares wearily at the table.

No one seems particularly interested in Primrose's explanation—although to be fair, "I went for a morning picnic and got lost in the woods" is pretty weak sauce. It seems more important for them to stress how terrified they were and how precious and fragile she is. "For one-and-twenty years I have sought only to protect you," the King says mournfully. "How could you risk yourself in this manner? Did you think nothing of our love for you?"

In that moment he reminds me of Charm's parents, or maybe my own: a person whose love is a burdensome thing, a weight dragging always at your ankles.

Primrose listens with a glassy, passive expression that tells me she's heard it many times before, has grown so used to the shackles around her legs that she barely feels them.

I make a small, involuntary sound somewhere between disgust and empathy. Prince Harold looks up. "And who is this?" His voice cuts through the King's speech. "She is not one of your ladies, I would swear it, and she is dressed most curiously."

It takes physical effort not to flip him off.

The princess's expression remains glassy, opaque. "This is the Lady Zinnia. I met her on my journey, and I am indebted to her for her courage against the perils we faced."

"There need not have *been* any perils if you'd stayed where you belong!" The King launches into another long speech about duty, family, fatherhood, honor, womanly virtues, and the obedience owed to one's elders and monarchs, but Prince Harold's eyes remain on me. His face is too lumpishly handsome to pull off *canny*, but there's a suspicious set to his mouth that I dislike.

Whatever. Soon enough I'll be home and his fiancée will be asleep, and none of his suspicions will matter.

Eventually the King blusters himself into silence and tells his daughter they'll discuss her punishment in the morning.

"Of course, Father," Primrose says placidly. Her eyes cut to her mother and for a moment the glass cracks. Her lips twist, her mouth half opens, but all she says is, "Good night, Mother." The Queen dips her head in a low, almost apologetic nod that makes me wonder if her love might not be quite so burdensome.

The two of us are escorted up to her rooms by a bustling flock of maids and ladies. The princess is fed and fussed over, pampered and cooed at, bathed and dressed in a nightgown so stiff with embroidery it can't possibly be comfortable. It's nearly midnight before they leave us alone.

Primrose climbs into that enormous, ridiculous bed, half swallowed by eiderdown and shadow. "You—you'll follow me, when I go?"

"Yeah." I consider the window seat or the carved chairs, then peel out of my hoodie and tennis shoes and crawl in bed after the princess. She doesn't move or speak, but I catch the wet gleam of her eyes in the dark, the silent slide of tears. I pretend I'm Charm, who knows how to comfort someone who can't be comforted. "Hey, it's okay, alright? I'll walk with you, every step. You won't be alone." We might not be able to fix our bullshit stories, but surely we can be less lonely inside them, here at the end. "Just go to sleep. I'm right here."

Her hand reaches into the space between us and I place my palm over it. We fall asleep curled toward one another like a pair of parentheses, like bookends on either side of the same shitty book.

❄   ❄   ❄

THE CURSE COMES for her in the fathomless black after midnight, but long before dawn. I wake to find the princess sitting up, her eyes open and vacant, foxfire green. She climbs out of bed like a sleepwalker, full of terrible, invisible purpose, and I pad behind her on bare feet.

The castle corridors are twistier and colder than I remember, with every torch doused and every door closed. The wind whips through narrow slits in the stone, tangling Primrose's hair and raising goosebumps on my arms as we wind down one corridor and up another, through a plain door I bet a million bucks didn't exist until just now. Behind it are stairs that spiral endlessly upward, lit by a sourceless, sickly light.

I don't need to tell you what happens next. You know how the story goes: the princess climbs the tower. The spinning wheel waits. She reaches one long, tapered finger toward it, her eyes faraway and faintly troubled, as if she's dreaming an unpleasant dream from which she can't wake.

The only difference is me. A second princess, crownless and greasy-haired, desperately in need of modern medicine and clean laundry, quietly crying in the shadows behind her. "Goodnight, princess," I whisper. She hesitates, the frown lines on her face deepening briefly before the fairy's enchantment smooths them away.

Her finger is an inch from the spindle's end when I hear a sound I've never heard in real life, but which I recognize from an adolescence spent rewatching *Lord of the Rings*: a sword being drawn from a scabbard. Then comes the ringing of boots on stairs, the drag of cloaks on stone, and armored men pour into the tower room.

A broad hand closes around Primrose's arm and hauls her backward. A silver blade crashes down on the spinning wheel and I flinch from flying splinters. I lower my arms to see a square-jawed man standing triumphantly above the shattered wreckage of the thing that was my only way home.

Prince Harold is panting lightly, his fingers still tight around Primrose's arm. He casts a heroic glance in her direction, a curl of hair falling artfully across his forehead. "You are safe, princess, do not fear."

Primrose doesn't look frightened. She looks baffled and bleary, distantly annoyed. Harold doesn't seem to notice. He raises his sword once more and points it directly at my chest. "Guards! Seize her!"

I have time for a single airless "*what the shit*" before my arms are wrenched behind me and my wrists are wrapped in cold iron. I writhe against the chains, but I can feel the weakness of my limbs, the stony strength of the men holding me.

Harold shakes his head at me, flicking that perfect curl from his forehead. "Did you think you could evade me twice, fairy?" He gestures imperiously to the tower steps. "To the dungeons."

7

THE DUNGEON ISN'T so much a place as a collection of generic dungeon-ish elements: damp stone walls and iron bars; dangling chains stained with God knows what; brittle bones piled in the corners, cracked and yellow; a decayed sweetness in the air, like a root cellar with something rotting in it.

In all my twenty-one years of bad luck, I don't think I've ever been this thoroughly, irredeemably fucked. I'm locked in a windowless cell in the wrong reality, wondering how long I can stay on my feet before I'm forced to sit on the stained stone floor. I'm hungry and thirsty and fatally ill. I have no way home. My only friend in this entire backwards-ass pre-Enlightenment world is about to be married off to a sentient cleft chin. Right now, the King is probably debating whether to drown me or burn me or make me dance in hot iron shoes.

I wanted to wrench my story off its tracks, to strike out toward some better ending, but all I've done is change my lines. I made myself the witch, and witches have even worse endings than princesses.

My therapist—who is corny and sincere, but usually right—says when things get overwhelming it can help to make a list of your assets. It's a short list: a small pile of vertebrae in the corner; a tin pail of unsanitary drinking water; several protein-clogged organs; a phone with approximately 12% of its battery life remaining.

I turn it on and scroll through my missed texts, because why not? There's no reason to hoard the charge now.

Charm's sent me a few more wild theories and links to NASA pages that don't load. I figure I have time to kill so I zoom in on the screenshots enough to read—well, skim—okay, *glance at*—the articles. All of them seem to subscribe to the (hypothetical, unprovable) concept of the multiverse, in which there are an infinite number of realities separated by nothing but a few quarks and cosmic dust bunnies. One dude describes them as bubbles in paint, endlessly spawning; somebody else asks me to envision a six-sided die that lands six different ways and spawns six alternate realities. My favorite is the one that describes the universe as "a vast book containing an infinity of pages." I like the idea that I'm just a misplaced punctuation mark or a straying verb who somehow found herself on the wrong page. Beats being a dice roll or a paint bubble.

I wish Charm were here to mock my lack of basic scientific understanding (when you skip half of high school and major in liberal arts, there are certain inevitable holes in your education). I always sort of imagined her beside me at the end, weeping prettily at my bedside, perhaps catching the eye of the extremely hot nurse who works the day shift in the ICU. Maybe they see each other again at my graveside and go out for drinks. Maybe they wind up married with three rescue dogs and a Subaru, who knows?

I type and delete several messages to Charm before going with the painfully effortful: bad news babe. portkey's busted.

that WOULD be bad news except—as I previously mentioned—portkeys are fiction

It takes less than ten seconds for me to send back a cropped version of one her own screenshots with the final line circled in red: "in a universe of infinite realities, there's no such thing as fiction."

She responds with a middle finger emoji, which is fair.

but like, real talk: the magic spinning wheel is broken. I think I might be stuck here forever. or for however long I have left. I've been trying not to feel the clogged-drain sensation in my chest or the shuddering weight of my own limbs, trying not to think of the X-rays that sent Mom straight out to her rose beds, her face cold and hard as a spade.

did you read the stuff I sent you?

of course, I lie.

There's a pause, then: if you had, which you definitely have not, you'd know that alternate dimensional realities are unlikely to be connected by individual physical objects.

charm please. I've had a real long day.

there are no ruby slippers or rabbit holes. if there's a way between universes, which there apparently is, it's something weirder and more quantum-y than a magic fucking spinning wheel. allow me to present my top ten theories thus far. I can see her so clearly: cross-legged in bed in the crappy two-room apartment she rented for the summer, surrounded by a small ocean of printed-out articles and library books and Smarties wrappers. The whole place would smell like burned coffee and laundry and weed, because Charm is essentially a frat boy with brains and breasts.

Her next text is an image of a PowerPoint slide titled, *So You Fucked Up and Got Lost in the Multiverse.* The subtitle reads: *Theory #1: narrative resonance,* followed by a pretty unreasonable number of bullet points.

How many jokey, stupid, helpful slideshows has she made me over the years? In junior year it was, *So You Want to Disappear: Ninety-Nine Reasons to Stick Around, Asshole.* In college she sent me, *So You Want to Murder Your Roommate: Practical Suggestions for Making it Look Like an Accident.*

I stare at the damp gray ceiling for a while before responding. i thought you grew out of trying to save me

jesus zin you're so stupid sometimes. hot, but stupid.

She texts again before I can type anything more than *hey—*

why do you think I majored in biochem? why am I interning at goddamn pfizer??? why was my senior thesis on MAL-09?

I know why. Just like I know why Dad still stays up too late reading message boards and googling unlikely medical experiments, why Mom still attends Roseville's Children meetings every month. Their love has hung above me like the sun, a burning brightness I could survive only if I never looked straight at it, never flew too close.

My phone buzzes again. i never stopped trying to save you. so don't you fucking dare stop trying to save yourself.

I stare, unblinking, the words fractured and blurred through the sheen of tears, and she adds: you promised to come back.

I shove the phone back in my jeans pocket and press the heels of my hands into my eyes hard enough that tiny fireworks pop against my eyelids. At sixteen, I tried to run away from my story and couldn't. So I put away my dreams of adventure and true love and happily ever afters, and settled in to play out the clock. I made my dying girl rules and followed them to the letter. I even wrote Charm a very serious three-page breakup letter and she informed me that (1) I was a dumbass, (2) you can't break up with your best friend, legally, and (3) she preferred blonds anyway.

And she stuck around. Through every doctor's appointment and prescription refill, every *Gargoyles* rewatch and whiny text about my roommate. I pity all those other Auroras and Briar Roses, the sleeping beauties who are alone in their little paint-bubble universes.

I wish I could bleed from my page to theirs, like ink. I wonder if that's more or less what I did. I wonder what happens when you tell the same story again and again in a thousand overlapping realities, like a pen retracing the same words over and over on the page. I wonder precisely what Charm meant by *narrative resonance*.

And then I have my second big, stupid, excellent idea. I retrieve my phone (8%) and write back to Charm: ok.

Then: i'm gonna need your help.

❀ ❀ ❀

THE FIRST GUARD who visits my cell is too scared of me to be any use at all. I badger him with questions and demands while he quivers and slides a bowl of greenish soup through the bars. He retreats back up the steps and I'm left to pace and scheme and consider all the many and varied ways this plan could fail. The soup congeals at my feet, like a pond scumming over.

The second guard is made of sterner stuff, refilling my water pail with hands that shake only slightly. He barely screams when I grab his wrist.

"Unhand me, foul creature!"

"I need to speak to the King."

"And why would our noble King consort with an unnatural—"

"Because I have a final request. Even unnatural creatures are owed some dignity in death, aren't they? Before they die?" I step closer to the bars as I say it, tilting my head upward and putting the slightest tremble in my lower lip. This is the exact fragile-wilting-flower act that got me out of at least 50 percent of my gym classes in high school.

I see the guard's throat bob. He is no longer trying quite so hard to remove his hand from mine. "I—I will pass your request along."

I let go of his wrist and sweep my eyelashes down. "Thank you, kind sir. And may I ask one question more?"

"You may." He's rubbing the place where my fingers held his wrist.

"The wedding. When will it be held?" Three days hence, the King had said, but that was seven days ago.

A suspicious line forms between the guard's brows, as if it's occurred to him that wicked fairies and weddings are an unfortunate combination. He must not be wholly convinced of my wickedness, because he says slowly, "Tomorrow, just after the dawn prayer."

"Thank you." I spread my fingers across my chest and sweep him the best curtsy I can achieve in unwashed jeans. He clunks into the wall on his way out of the dungeon.

I return to my unproductive pacing and scheming, stopping only to cough up weird, mucus-y lumps that I try not to look at very closely. If there were X-rays in this world, I bet my chest would look like a galaxy, the healthy black peppered with white stars of protein.

Hours pass. The King never arrives.

But someone else comes in his place. She descends the steps slowly, velvet skirts dragging across stained stone, rings shining hard and bright on her fingers.

The Queen stands on the other side of the bars, entirely alone, watching me down her too-long nose. There's a steely chill in her eyes that makes it clear that my long-lashed, damsel-in-distress persona will get me exactly nowhere. I should have known Primrose's spine didn't come from her father.

I open with a grave "Your Majesty" instead. The Queen doesn't so much as blink. I wet my cracked lips. "I would like to make a final request."

"And why should I grant you any requests?" Her tone is so perfectly calm that I see giant flashing warning lights ahead. It's the voice Mom uses on doctors who talk down to me or school administrators who give her shit about all my absences.

"Because," I begin carefully, but the Queen cuts me off in the same flat voice.

"Why should I grant anything at all to the creature who cursed my daughter?"

"Because I'm someone's daughter too, whatever else you think I am." God, what if this doesn't work? What if I vanish from my parents' world and leave them with a terrible absence in place of an ending? Running away had seemed so romantic when I was a kid, but I'd planned to leave a note, at least. "And my mother wouldn't want me to spend my last night surrounded by filth and darkness."

Something flashes behind the Queen's eyes, red and wounded, before she banishes it. "It is our choices which determine our fates. Each of us gets what we deserve."

"Oh, *bullshit*."

"How *dare* you—"

"I'm sorry. I meant: bullshit, *Your Majesty*. Did your daughter choose to be cursed? Did she choose to marry that dumbass prince?"

The Queen seethes at me, that red wound glistening behind her eyes. "There are certain duties—certain responsibilities that come with her rank and birth—"

Watching her choke with rage, a sudden suspicion occurs to me. I lean closer to the bars. "Did you *choose* to marry the King? Or would you have chosen differently for yourself, if you could? If this world permitted you to?"

The Queen is silent, her face wracked with rage or despair or maybe both. I can't tell whether she's considering helping me or setting me on fire herself. But why did she come down here without handmaidens or ladies or even guards? Why did she answer my call at all? Perhaps she, too, is hoping for a last-second miracle.

"Listen." I whisper it, one conspirator to another. "Give me what I need, and I might be able to help her. I might be able to give your daughter the first real choice she's had in her life."

The Queen stares at me for a very long time. In her face I see the cold weight of the choices she didn't have and the chances she didn't take, the weary years waiting for fate to swallow her daughter the same way it swallowed her. I see her choosing now whether to make her love into a cage or a key.

She smooths her palms down the rich velvet of her gown and asks, quite matter-of-factly, "What do you require?"

✺ ✺ ✺

THE ROSES ARRIVE by the bucket and barrelful, carried by bewildered guards and skeptical gardeners. They must have stripped every climbing vine and rosebush for miles, tying the flowers into hasty bundles and hauling them down to the dungeons to fulfill the fairy's final request. They must think I've gone mad; they might be right.

By the time the last footsteps echo back up the stairs, my cell looks like a poorly tended greenhouse: roses burst from every corner, lining the walls and pressing through the bars. Fallen petals carpet the floor. The air smells green and sweet and bright, like summer. Like home.

I lie on the hard stone, the dampness leaching through my jeans, the petals clinging to the bare backs of my arms. I check my phone to see if Charm wrote back, if she made it to the tower, if the roses are still there—but it makes a final, weary bleat and the screen goes dark.

After that there's nothing to do but fall asleep. I tell myself a fairy tale, the way I did when I was little, imagining a great unseen pen retracing the same letters over and over, the ink bleeding through to the next page.

I begin at the end: *Once upon a time there was a princess who slept surrounded by roses.*

8

I DON'T KNOW when I start dreaming, or whether it's a dream at all. What do you call the vast nothing between the pages of the universe? The whisper-thin nowhere-at-all that waits in the place where one story ends and another begins?

The world smears sideways around me. A silent wind rushes past.

I see a woman sleeping in a castle bedroom, its windows dark with thorns.

I see a woman sleeping on a mountaintop, broad-shouldered and armored, surrounded by shields and flames. Her nose is crooked and scarred; she scowls even in her sleep.

I see a woman sleeping in a chrome coffin, white frost prickling across the deep brown of her skin. There is nothing but a thin metal hull between her and the star-strewn black of space.

I see a woman sleeping among the wild roses of the deep woods, her hair cropped short and her hand curled around the hilt of a sword.

I see women sleeping in towers and townhouses, attics and lakes, hospital beds and spaceships. Some of them sleep serenely, as if they've accepted their fate; some of them look like they fought fate tooth and nail and are still ready to go another round. All of them are alone.

Except me, because I have Charm. I see her sleeping on top of a grubby comforter in the abandoned guard tower on Route 32. The buckets and vases of roses still surround her, their edges curled black with age, their leaves shriveled. The bleached wing of her hair is fanned like a halo behind her head and there's a misshapen tutu tugged over her jeans. The plastic crown she gave me on my birthday glimmers false gold on her brow. I told her to dress like a princess, and I guess this is as close as she gets.

I'm so relieved to see her I almost wake from this not-quite dream. I wasn't sure it would work—Charm isn't really a sleeping beauty. But she had a mother and father who longed for a daughter, and she shared my curse with me for almost twenty-one years. And she climbed to the top of the tallest tower in the land and slept surrounded by roses. It must have been enough.

Or maybe—I look at her hand, still curled tight around her phone, still waiting for my next text—we're so much a part of one another's stories that the laws of physics bend for us, just a little.

Charm opens her eyes. I see my name on her lips. Her hand reaches up toward me and I reach down to her, and I know, I *know*, that I could step out of this knockoff fairy tale world and go back into my own. I could go home, and to hell with Primrose and Prince Harold and shitty medieval gender roles.

But I promised the Queen I would try to change her daughter's fate, and I promised Primrose she wouldn't be alone. And maybe the dying girl rules are garbage, and instead of just trying not to die we should be trying to live.

My hand finds Charm's and I haul her toward me. I feel her body land beside mine on the dungeon floor, smell the slightly chemical citrus of her hair, but I remain in the whirling in-between. I look out at all those hundreds of sleeping beauties, trapped and cursed, bound and buried, all alone. I wonder if they'll even be able to hear me, and if any of them will answer; I wonder how badly they want out of their stories.

The void between worlds is nibbling at my edges, tearing at my borders. I don't know what'll happen if I linger too long, but I imagine it's the same thing that would happen to a chickadee who lingered in a jet engine. I reach my hand out to all the sleeping princesses and whisper the word that brought me into Primrose's world, that sent both our stories careening off their tracks: "*Help.*"

I land back on the cold cell of my floor, surrounded by roses and rot. My last bleary thought before I slip into true sleep, or possibly a coma, is that some of the beauties must have heard me.

Because some of them have answered.

❋ ❋ ❋

HANDS ARE SHAKING my shoulders. A voice—a voice I know better than any other voice in the world—is saying my name. "Zinnia Gray. I did not zap myself into another dimension to watch you die. Wake *up.*"

I open my eyes to the same face I've woken up to on hundreds of Saturday mornings since second grade: Charmaine Baldwin. She's looming over me with a worried frown and wild hair. I give her a lopsided smile. "Morning, sunshine."

She rests her forehead very briefly against mine. "Oh, thank Jesus."

I sit up slowly, achy and stiff, feeling simultaneously hungover and still drunk, to find that my list of assets has expanded considerably while I slept: there are now four women crammed into my narrow, rose-filled cell.

Charm, sitting cross-legged with her tutu crumpled in her lap and her head tilted back against the bars, eyes closed in relief. The short-haired girl with the sword and the stubborn jaw who reminds me of every young adult protagonist from the '90s; the Black space princess wearing a silvery suit and a skeptical expression, stepped straight out of science fiction; the armored Viking woman whose name is probably something like Brunhilda and whose shoulders are wider than any three of us shoved together.

All of them came when I called. All of them stepped out of their own narratives to save someone else. All of them are staring at me.

"Uh," I begin auspiciously. "Thank you all for coming." I'm banking on the fairy tale logic of this world to let them understand me. "I think you're all—well, I think we're all versions of the same story, retold in different realities. The universe is like a book, see, and telling a story is like writing on a page. And if a story is told enough times, the ink bleeds through." Charm makes a small, pained sound at the scientific absurdity of my explanation. The other beauties stare at me in unblinking unison.

"So we're . . . the ink? In this metaphor?" It's the space princess, whose expression of skepticism has deepened by several degrees.

"Yes?"

Charm rescues me, as usual. "Don't we have a wedding to stop? A princess to save?"

"Oh, right. So there's another one of us here. She was cursed to prick her finger on a spindle's end and fall into a hundred-year sleep"—a series of grim nods from the other beauties—"except it turns out the curse was supposed to save her from a shitty marriage"—at least two grim nods—"and she's probably standing at the altar right now. I was hoping you could help me bust out of here and save her."

A painful silence follows while they exchange a series of glances. The '90s heroine-type cocks her head at me. "And afterward you'll send us home?"

"Or wherever else you want to go." Assuming I can arrange another moment of sufficient narrative resonance, but I elect not to alarm them with the sketchy details of my sketchy-ass plan.

The Viking woman gives a wordless shrug, tosses her pale braids over one shoulder, and turns to face the barred door. She wraps her scarred fists around the bars and muscle ripples across her back. Ropes of tendon twist down her arms.

I have time to think *no fucking way* before the iron gives a long groan of submission. The bars are warping beneath her fists, bending slowly inward, when a blue bolt of light streaks past my ear. It sizzles through the iron like spit through tissue paper, leaving nothing but a ragged, faintly smoking hole where the latch used to be. The Viking lets go of the bars. The door swings meekly open.

We turn collectively toward the space princess, who is holstering something shiny and chrome that's probably called a blaster or a plasma arc. I hear Charm whisper a reverent *hot damn*.

We ascend the stairs in single file, boots and tennis shoes and bare feet tapping against the stone. A pair of guards wait at the top, hands slack around their spears, entirely unprepared for a legion of renegade princesses to descend upon them like a set of mismatched Valkyries.

In less than ten seconds Brunhilda and the girl with the sword have them kneeling, disarmed, and gibbering, their own weapons leveled at their throats. I lean down and give a small wave. "Hi, sorry. Where's the chapel? We've got a happily ever after to stop."

There's a queasy second where I think they might pass out before answering, but one of them swallows against his own spearpoint and raises a shaking finger. I thank them both sincerely before Brunhilda clangs their helmets together like brass bells. They slump against the wall and I think a little giddily of the versions of this story where the castle falls asleep with its princess, from kings to cooks to the mice in the walls.

Charm takes off down the corridor and I follow, and then the five of us are flying, running down toward the wedding like last chances or last-second miracles, like twist endings in a story you've heard too many times.

        ❁ ❁ ❁

LOGICALLY WE COULD show up at the ceremony at the wrong time: ten minutes too early, when guests are still filing into the pews, or half an hour too late, when the chapel is emptying and the princess has already been swept away by her uncharming prince.

But we're in a fairy tale, and fairy tales have a logic all their own.

We skid around a final corner and see a pair of arched doors standing open. Ceremonial-sounding Latin drifts through them, echoing off stone walls. I tiptoe to the doorway and peer around the corner. The room is smaller than I expected, with a dozen rows of pews lined up beneath a vaulted ceiling. Morning light falls through a single circular window, gilding the bride and groom on the dais below.

Princess Primrose looks literally divine, Boticelli's Venus with clothes. Her hair is burnished gold beneath the thinnest whisper of a veil; her gown is a rich rose the precise shade of her lips. Her face is coldest ivory.

Prince Harold looks ridiculous. He's wearing those embarrassing medieval pants that poof out above the knee and he's looking at Primrose the way a man might look at his favorite golf club, fondly possessive.

Charm pokes her head around me and gives a silent whistle. "That's her, huh?"

"Yeah." I pull back from the doorway and chew my lip. "I can't remember if they did the 'speak now or forever hold your peace' thing in medieval times, or if it's one of those Victorian inventions, like brides wearing white, or homophobia. Should we wait and see or—"

But Charm isn't listening, because Charm is already moving. She strolls through the chapel doors and down the aisle like a fashion model with a bad attitude, a deus ex machina in black jeans. "Hey!" Her voice shouts back at the congregation from the arched ceiling, redoubled. The Latin chanting stops abruptly. Charm slides her hands into her pockets and shrugs one shoulder, her chin high. "I object. Or whatever."

The silence is broken only by the slide of satin as the gathered lords and ladies swivel in their seats to look at Charm. The Superman tattoo grins back at them.

Primrose turns slowly on the dais, her face filling with a desperate, painful hope, the kind of hope that has died at least once and is rising now from its own ashes. Her eyes fall on Charm and the hope ignites, blazing hot.

I look past the princess to the throne where her mother sits. The Queen looks suitably shocked, her hand held primly before her open mouth, but behind the shock I see an echo of the same hope that burns in her daughter's face, like reflected flames.

The guards stir against the walls, their polished armor clanking awkwardly. I guess guard training doesn't cover bleached blonds interrupting royal weddings, because they all look helplessly up at the dais for direction.

The King recovers his voice. "What are you waiting for? Seize this trespasser!"

I nod to the other beauties still hesitating with me, just outside the door. "That's our cue, ladies." The '90s heroine tosses me a spear she stole from the dungeon guards and braces her sword crosswise. The space princess draws her blaster and does something complicated with the dials and buttons on the side. Brunhilda cracks her neck to one side and gives me a small, ominous smile.

We pour into the chapel after Charm, a horde of misfits bristling with weapons. I swing my spear with all the enthusiasm my scrawny, oxygen-starved muscles can muster, which isn't much, but it doesn't seem to matter—the guards are so thoroughly taken aback by our arrival they appear frozen in place, their jaws hanging loose.

"Primrose, come on!" The princess gathers her vast skirts in two hands and makes it one step down the dais before Prince Harold catches her wrist. The fabric of her sleeve puckers beneath his grip, crushed tight.

Primrose spins back to face him, golden hair arcing behind her, crown askew. The perfect porcelain princess has vanished, replaced by someone angrier and wearier and far less inclined to tolerate bull-shit. "Let go of me," she spits.

If Harold had the sense God gave a dachshund, he would listen to her. He doesn't.

Primrose closes her eyes very briefly, either gathering herself or abandoning herself, before she punches him in the face. I don't know much about hand-to-hand combat, but it's pretty clear that she's never punched anyone in the face before. It's equally clear that Prince Harold has never been punched. He reels back with a profoundly un-manly squeal, releasing her wrist to press both hands to his face and bleat.

Primrose looks sick and giddy as she turns away, even paler than usual. Her feet tangle in the vast drape of her own dress and she topples forward, but Charm is somehow already at her side, arms out-stretched. She catches the princess as she falls, a knight catching a swooning damsel in a cheesy Hollywood movie.

Charm looks down at Primrose, her arm wrapped tight around her waist, and Primrose looks up at her, one hand resting delicately on her breastbone. The two of them remain that way so long I suspect they've forgotten the crowded chapel around us,

the impending guards, everything in all the infinite universes except one another. I don't know if I believe in love at first sight in
the real world, but we're not in the real world, are we?

I break away from the other beauties to flick the back of Charm's
head. "Let's go, huh?"

"Right." Charm detaches herself with some difficulty and leads
Primrose by the hand. I linger long enough to glance up at the Queen
and give her a final, unmilitary salute. She nods infinitesimally back,
a captain remaining with her ship.

I'm turning away when Prince Harold says, his voice thick and
fleshy through his swollen nose, "I don't understand." His eyes are
on Primrose and Charm, on the place where their hands are joined
together so tightly they look like a single creature.

"Well, Harold," I say gently. "They're lesbians." The Prince stares
back at me with the dull, suspicious squint of a man who has been
mocked on previous occasions by words he doesn't know.

"Guards!" The King bellows again, but whatever order he's about
to issue is interrupted by a soft gasp from the Queen. She appears
to have fainted, contriving to drape herself perfectly across her husband's lap.

It would be a shame to waste whatever seconds she's bought us. I
join my fellow sleeping beauties and we make our way back down the
aisle surrounded by the blue sizzle of blaster fire and the clang of blade
against blade. Some brighter-than-average guard has drawn and barred
the chapel door, entirely failing to calculate the breadth of Brunhilda's
shoulders or the circumference of her biceps. She barely breaks her
stride as she crashes through it.

The five of us rush into the hallway and I grab the princess's sleeve.
"Primrose! We need to get back to the tower. Can you lead us there?"

"I-I don't know. I'm not asleep, so I don't know if the curse—"

"You were always fighting it before, right? So it could only take hold of you when you were sleeping. Now I need you to *stop* fighting."

Primrose looks like she's considering telling me that's not how it works, that it's impossible, but she pauses. Her eyes flick around to the four interdimensional sleeping beauties gathered around her, armed with swords and spears and space-blasters, and I watch her recalculate her definition of what is and isn't possible.

She closes her eyes. Charm gives her hand a small, encouraging squeeze.

I didn't realize how tense she was, how constantly on guard, until I watch her let it all go. Her shoulders fall. Her arms loosen at her sides. When she opens her eyes, they're the deep, haunted green of undersea caves.

She looks at each of us in turn, dreamy, almost drunk. "Follow me."

9

WE FOLLOW HER. Up staircases and down corridors, running through deep pools of shadow and beams of dust-specked sunlight, cries of alarm sounding behind us.

I run with the others at first. But something's gone tight and funny in my chest, as if my organs are held in a pair of clumsy fists. My lungs are sacks of wet sand and my pulse is a clock tick-tocking in my ears. *Not now*, I plead with it. *Please, give me a little more time*.

I would laugh at myself if I had the breath to spare. It's what I've always wanted, what I'll never get.

My legs weaken, starved of blood and breath. The other beauties stream past me and I wheeze behind them, too breathless to call for help, even to swear. The gap between us widens. They round a corner ahead and I'm deciding whether to limp faster or rest for a moment against this friendly-looking wall when I hear Charm's voice say, "Everybody hold the fuck up. Where's Zin?"

I lean against the wall, letting the chill of the stones seep through my T-shirt. A vast pair of boots appears in my vision. "Oh, hi Brunhilda. If that's your . . . actual . . ." I have to pause mid-sentence to gulp air. I'm not a medical professional, but that seems like a not-great sign. ". . . name."

"It is Brünhilt." A hand settles on my shoulder, wide and warm. "May I?" It's the first time I've heard her speak. Her voice is surprisingly high, like a hawk calling in the distance.

I'm pretty sure I nod because the next thing I feel is a pair of arms gathering me up and armor grating against my cheek. My body jars with every step but the pain is harmless, almost pleasant, compared to the ache in my chest. Bruises fade, after all.

Charm's worried face swims above me. "Zin?"

"It's fine," I assure her, but my breath whistles weirdly in my throat. She doesn't look comforted.

Clanging sounds echo up the corridor, booted feet and armored legs moving closer. "Let's just go, okay?" I don't hear Charm's answer, but Brünhilt starts moving again. I try to look up once or twice to see how close the guards are and whether we're going fast enough, but everything jounces and rattles and hurts so I give up, lolling against Brünhilt instead. There's a soupy, suffocating lethargy spreading from my extremities, inching up my limbs, tugging me toward sleep.

I tell myself a story to stay awake. *Once upon a time there was a princess cursed to sleep for a hundred years.*

I open my eyes and catch the blurred gleam of Primrose's hair as she leads us up the winding tower steps, her spine stiff and her crown high, a princess refusing to go gently into her own good night.

Once upon a time she asked for help.

And I answered her. All of us did. We followed the lonely threads of our stories across the vast nothing of the universe and found our way here, to this tower, to save at least one princess from her curse. I've always resented people for trying to save me, but maybe this is how it works, maybe we save one another.

I become aware that Brünhilt has stopped climbing just before Charm says, tentatively, "Zin?" I try to respond but succeed only in making a sound like a plunger in a clogged sink. "Was there supposed to be something up here? Like, say, a spinning wheel?" Charm's voice is strung tight.

I struggle out of Brünhilt's arms and stand on fizzing, trembling legs. Her hand hovers at my back, ready to catch me, and I don't trust myself enough to pull away. I blink around the tower room. There's nothing but smooth flagstones and five sleeping beauties, their expressions reflecting five variations of "Now what, bitch?"

There's no spinning wheel. Even the busted remains of the one Harold smashed are gone, neatly swept away by some fastidious guard. Shouldn't it have magically reconstituted itself in our absence? My plan was to prick my finger on something and fall asleep and hope that was enough to send us back into the whirling multiverse—but what the hell am I going to do now?

Distantly, I hear the thudding of boots on the winding tower steps. We don't have long, and if we're captured there won't be any secret pacts or miraculous escapes. I picture the '90s heroine forced into skirts and deprived of her sword; Brünhilt in chains; the space princess peeled out of her chrome and silver armor, stuck forever on a single planet rather than sailing among the stars. Primrose, trapped in her silk sheets; Charm, unable to save her.

I wanted to save us all from our stories, but I should have known better than anybody: there are worse endings than sleeping for a hundred years.

Pain pops in my kneecaps, sharp and sudden. My teeth clack together. It's only when I hear Charm swearing that I realize I've fallen to the floor. I feel her arm bracing my shoulders, Primrose kneeling at my other side. I want to tell them I'm sorry, that I tried my best, but the tightness in my chest is suffocating me. My pulse has lost its steady tick-tocking rhythm, thundering like hooves in my ears. Darkness nibbles at the edges of my vision.

The floor tilts toward me, or maybe I tilt toward the floor, and then my cheek is plastered against cold stone. I blink once, staring hazily at the boots and slippers and bare feet of the beauties around me. I guess I get a theatrical death after all, sprawled at the top of the tallest tower, pale and fragile as any Rackham princess, but a lot less lonely.

I see it in the half second before my eyes hinge shut: a slender shard lying on the floor. A single splinter of dark wood that might once have belonged to a spindle. *It wasn't a spinning wheel in the original version.*

I feel my lips peeling back over my teeth in a bloodless smile. I've

read enough fantasy novels to recognize a last chance when I see one. This is the part where I rally my final strength, calling on reserves of fortitude I didn't know I had to reach my numb fingers for that splinter. With my dying breath I will prick my finger and pull us all into the space between stories, and all the beauties will weep with gratitude and admiration as they escape into whatever new narratives they choose, and I will fall into my final sleep knowing I've done something worthwhile—

Except I don't have any secret reserves of strength. There's no amount of conviction or hope or love that can keep my overstuffed heart from stopping or my oxygen-starved brain from going gray.

My hand barely brushes the splinter when my vision turns the final, empty black of a theater screen just before the credits roll. I feel myself falling down, down into the kind of sleep that has no dreams and never ends.

The last thing I hear is my own name, spoken in a voice that sounds like a heart breaking. The last thing I think is how ironic it is, how fucking hilarious, that Charm should spend her life trying to save me, and I should die trying to save her, and both of us would fail.

10

I FIGURE I'M dead. Again.

True, there's a grayish light glowing through my
eyelids and stiff sheets beneath my skin, but I chalk
that up to the random sensory misfirings of a dying
brain. Ditto for the soft squeaking of orthopedic tennis shoes on waxed floors and the distant beeps of
machines. It's the smell I can't seem to ignore: hand
sanitizer and human suffering. Surely no version of
heaven has hospital rooms.

I open my eyes. There's a paneled ceiling above
me. A whiteboard with the name of my nurse and
a smiley face written in blue marker. The intrusive
chill of oxygen tubing beneath my nose and the
prickle of an IV in the crook of my arm. The window is one of those unopenable, industrial affairs,
nothing at all like the arrow slit of a castle tower.

I know my regional hospital rooms: I'm in the
ICU of Riverside Methodist Hospital on the north
side of Columbus.

It occurs to me that one explanation for the

seven days I spent trapped in a fairy tale is that I collapsed on the night of my twenty-first birthday and have spent the past week hooked up to an IV, furiously hallucinating about hot princesses and un-wicked fairies. That maybe I'm actually in one of those bullshit Wizard of Oz stories where the girl wakes up in the final chapter and everyone assures her it was all a dream.

But then—why is there a slender splinter of wood held tight in my fist? I press my thumb against my own fingertips, feeling for blood or bruises; there are none.

"Hey, hon." The words are rough with exhaustion, cracked with relief.

How many times have I woken in a hospital bed to the sound of my father's voice? How many times have I turned my stiff neck to see my parents perched at my bedside with new worry lines carved into their faces, cardboard cups of watery coffee clutched in their hands?

"Hey." My voice sounds like it's coming from inside a rusted pipe organ, a flaky wheeze. "Where's my Prince Charming?" It's the same joke I always make when I wake up from my surgeries and procedures. Usually Dad pulls a wounded, "Am I not charming?" face and Mom rolls her eyes and tousles his hair in a way that tells me she, at least, is thoroughly charmed.

This time they both burst into tears. Dad is the established crier of the family—he was asked to "get a grip or leave the theater" during the last twenty minutes of *Coco*—but this time Mom is crying just as hard, her shoulders heaving, her knuckles pressed to her eyes.

"Hey," I offer rustily. "Hey." And then somehow they're both on the bed next to me and our foreheads are mashed together and I'm crying too. I spent the last week (or maybe the last five years) trying not to let the weight of their love suffocate me. It doesn't feel very suffocating right now.

I clutch them a little closer, tucking my head into the hollow place right beneath Dad's collarbone the way I did when I was little, when my death was far away and neither of us were very afraid of it. We stay like that for a while, shuddering and snuffling at one another, Mom smoothing the hair from my forehead.

Questions intrude, scrolling gently across my brain like the banners behind planes at the beach. How did I get here? How am I not dead? Am I still dying?

I don't really care about most of them. There's only one thing (five things, technically) I care about. I pull back from my parents. "Is Charm around? Or . . ." I don't know how I'm going to finish that sentence—*or any other mythical figures/Disney princesses?*—but I don't have to.

The curtain between my bed and the next is flung back with a dramatic flourish, and there she is: five-and-a-half feet of attitude, a bleeding heart with bleached hair. Charm. She gives me a smile that's aiming for cavalier and landing closer to desperately relieved, then tugs someone else around the curtain. She's tall and slender, with enormous eyes and fragile wrists that extend several inches beyond the sleeves of Charm's leather jacket. It takes me far too long to recognize her.

"*Primrose?* How—"

A helpless, giddy smile slides across the princess's face as Charm swaggers to the foot of the bed and sits casually on my ankles. "Morning, love."

A throat clears on the other side of the curtain and someone says, "There's a three-visitor limit, folks!" in the

cheery, steely tone of a nurse on a twelve-hour shift who is not interested in a single ounce of back talk.

Mom and Dad stand. "We'll give you all a minute," Dad stage-
whispers, and they edge around my princesses and out into the hall,
taking their cardboard cups with them.

I push the button that buzzes my bed upright. "Hi."

"Hi," Primrose answers carefully. "How are you?" She sounds like a
tourist who has memorized the local phrases from a guidebook.

I resettle the oxygen tubing beneath my nose. "Alive. So, you
know. Pretty excellent." As I say it, I realize it's true: I'm tired and a
little stiff, but my heart is thumping steadily in my ears and my lungs
are filling and emptying easily, casually, as if they could keep doing it
forever. Hope flutters again in my chest, a habit I can't seem to quit.
"How did we get back?"

"You fell into an accursed sleep," Primrose answers seriously. I guess
that's fairy tale–speak for *a hypoxic coma brought on by advanced amyloidosis.* "And I . . ." Primrose blushes and I find myself mesmerized by
the blotchy fuchsia of her cheeks; I hadn't thought it was possible for
her to look anything less than perfect.

"And she *kissed* you. You!" Charm shakes her head in mock disgust.
"Which was enough to trigger the narrative resonance between universes, I guess. Apparently fairy tales are flexible about gender roles."

A cursed girl sleeping in a tower; an heir to a throne bending to
kiss her. And if the heir was a princess instead of a prince, and if it's
more like awkward sexual tension between them than true love, well,
stories are told all sorts of ways, aren't they?

I run my thumb along the splinter in my hand, the slender last
hope which had done exactly nothing to save me. "And the others?
What happened to them?"

Charm makes a mystical woo-woo gesture with her fingers. "They took their exits on the cosmic highway between worlds, man." I kick her and she relents. "We all got sucked together into this whirling darkness—the void between universes, I guess—and the other princesses each chose a story to step into. The cryogenic space lady and the Viking lady went home, I think, but the short-haired girl with the sword went elsewhere. She struck me as the adventurous type." I picture her crashing headlong into some other unsuspecting sleeping beauty, a headstrong protagonist out to wreak merry havoc, and feel a weird lurch of something in my stomach. Regret, maybe, or envy.

Primrose finishes the story. "Charmaine took you to this world, and I followed. We landed in the tower of an abandoned castle"—the guard tower of the state penitentiary, I assume—"and Charmaine summoned assistance"—called an ambulance?—"because you wouldn't wake up. I thought for a time that you might be . . ." *Dead.*

"Yeah, me too," I tell her. "I will be soon, statistically." I try to say it with a shrug in my voice, the way I used to, but I can't quite pull it off. There's still a hot spark of hope caught in my chest, scorching my throat.

Charm frowns at me. Tilts her head. "Didn't they tell you?" she asks, and the hope catches fire. I can't speak, can't breathe, can hardly think around the bonfire of my own desire, twenty-one years of suppressed hunger for *more*: more life, more time, more everything. For the first time in my life I let myself believe I might, somehow, be cured.

Right up until Charm says, "I mean, it's not like you're cured or anything, but—" and the fire goes out like an ember beneath a boot. I don't hear the rest of Charm's sentence because I'm busy wishing I could rewind the world and linger in the radiant ignorance of two seconds ago, when I thought my story had finally changed. It's a good thing I already used up my tears for the year.

I stare fixedly, carefully at the wall as Charm stands and shuffles through a pile of folders and clipboards on the bedside table. She produces an oversized sheet of plastic and waves it in front of me. "It's still pretty rad, don't you think?" Her voice is soft but shaking with some enormous emotion, barely contained. Joy?

I look at the X-ray in her hands. For a long second I can't tell what I'm seeing; it's been years since I've seen my lungs without the white knots and tangles of proteins inside them. Now there's nothing but ghostly lines of ribs hovering above velvety darkness, clean and empty, just like the pictures of healthy lungs in Charm's textbooks.

She holds up a series of smaller photos beside it. Ultrasounds. I see my heart, my liver, my kidneys. A caption in blocky capitals reads *Findings: normal.*

I stare at the images for two seconds, then three. I blink. "I don't understand." My voice is a whisper.

"Zin—the proteins are gone. All the stuff that's been accumulating in your organs is just . . ." Charm snaps her fingers. "The doctors checked your identity like four extra times because they were sure you couldn't be the same girl. They have no idea how it happened."

She gives a smug little toss of her bangs that makes me ask, "But you do?"

Charm smiles at me with the gleeful enthusiasm that usually precedes a science lecture. "Well, I have a theory. I think when you travel to another dimension—which is a *real thing* that happened to *us*, by the way—the laws of physics, of reality itself, bend to match that universe."

"I thought the laws of physics never bent. I thought that's why we call them laws."

Charm sniffs. "Well, maybe they're more what you'd call guidelines, than actual laws. Anyway, the rules of Prim's world are different than ours." My brain, which is still processing the immensity of those clean X-rays, pauses to waggle its eyebrows and say, *Prim, eh?* "In her world there are wicked fairies and magic knives and probably unicorns. In her world, kisses lift curses."

I mull this over for another string of seconds. "But not in this one, huh?"

Some of the fervor leaks out of Charm's face. "No, not in this one. They took about fifty samples and confirmed that your RNA is still fucked. You are still officially diagnosed with Generalized Roseville Malady."

I picture the rules of this world reasserting themselves over my cells, harsh reality swallowing fantasy. I glance sideways at Primrose and understand that it's not just the leather jacket that confused me when I first saw her: her hair is an ordinary blond rather than a shimmering, impossible gold; her eyes are blue rather than cerulean; I think she might even have pores. She isn't a fairy tale princess any longer.

Charm clears her throat and slides the X-rays back into their stack. "But like, this is pretty good. *Very* good. It's like the clock is reset."

I swallow, tasting the plasticky cold of the artificial oxygen in my throat. "So—so how long—?" It's not a question I'm accustomed to asking. I've always known exactly how long I had left.

"They don't know," Charm answers. "It could be a month. It could be another twenty-one years. Welcome to regular-old mortality, friend." Her voice is shaking again and her eyes are shimmering with tears she's too stubborn to shed. Normally this is the point when I would look away from her, when the two of us would retreat to sarcasm and bravado. But God, I'm tired of being too cowardly to let myself love anyone. I catch her wrist and haul her toward me. She falls against my chest and I wrap my arms around her and it turns out I haven't used up my tears after all.

The princess steps around the bed and looks politely out the window while we cry at one another. I rub Charm's back and watch Primrose through the rainbowed distortion of tears. A princess who slept with a poison knife beneath her pillow, who rode into the night to face her own villain, who stands now in the strange light of a new world, unflinching. I don't think the next person Charm falls for will be a coward.

I scrub a hand across my cheeks and tousle Charm's hair. "You're snotting all over my hospital gown, hon."

She slides her gross face across my collarbone and burrows in a little closer. "Fuck off."

"So, *Prim*," I say loudly, "What do you think?"

The princess looks away from the window, a tendril of yellow hair drifting fetchingly in the air conditioning. "Of what?"

"Of our world." I gesture grandly at the cramped room, with its bland furniture and wipe-able surfaces. "It gets better than the Columbus ICU, I swear to god. There's . . . ice cream? Bet your world didn't have that. And dresses with pockets. Gay rights, at least some places." Charm goes very still against my chest, barely breathing. "You wouldn't be a princess anymore, but you're hot and white and young, so you could be pretty much anything else you wanted. A librarian or a physical therapist or a lion tamer, if those are still a thing." I can see the idea taking hold of Primrose, rising like stars in her eyes. A whole galaxy of possibilities laid out where before there had been a single, narrow story with a single, bitter end. I know precisely how she feels. "Would you like to stay?"

Charm sits up. She looks at Primrose and then away, as if she doesn't care what the answer is. Charm's worst crushes are generally the ones she pretends she doesn't have.

Primrose is looking down at her borrowed clothes, running her thumb along the leather sleeve of her jacket. Her hand is shaking. "Could I?"

I kick Charm again and she clears her throat. "Yeah. I mean, you could stay at my place. I mostly sleep on the couch anyway." This is a stone-cold lie, but I don't call her on it. Some lies are important.

Primrose looks at Charm through her lashes. I see her eyes trace the stubborn line of her chin, the defiant square of her shoulders. "I—yes. I would like that." Charm gives her a watery, puffy-eyed smile, and Primrose smiles back, and I'm torn between rolling my eyes at them and crying some more.

Primrose unglues herself from Charm with an almost audible snapping sound and turns to me, that silly smile still in place. "And what about you? What will you do?"

I open my mouth to answer, but nothing comes out. I just stare back at her, jaw loose, feeling all those galaxies of possibilities spinning around me. I've never thought about the future. I never had one.

Charm's hand finds mine and squeezes. I squeeze back. "I don't know," I answer, and it's the simple, glorious truth.

11

It takes me about three weeks to figure it out.

I spend the time bouncing between home and the hospital and Charm's place. I don't actually need to be in the hospital. The doctors tell me the first few globules of protein have appeared in my organs, but I still feel better than I have in years, and there's still nothing they can do but hand me some steroids and suppressants to slow it down. Mostly I think they just want to continue poking and prodding at me. They keep scheduling me for more samples and tests and biopsies, followed by interviews with panels of doctors whose attitudes have moved from baffled to ambitious, as if they're seeing themselves presenting their findings to packed lecture halls, using laser pointers to circle my miraculously empty lungs. I should be worried about transitioning from dying girl to lab rat, but I can't seem to be worried about anything. And I already know—in a wordless, formless way—that I'm not sticking around.

Between appointments I'm mostly at Charm's place, which is conspicuously less disastrous than it used to be. There are even curtains on the windows now, instead of towels held up with binder clips; I would worry about what this means in terms of how hard she's falling for Prim, except that Prim seems to be falling just as fast. The first time I show up she tells me about the Swiss Army knife Charm gave her with a degree of sappiness generally reserved for bouquets or diamond rings. "It's *mine*! Charm says I don't even need to hide it!" I can't believe how much I missed those exclamation points. "It's a tool *and* a weapon!"

"Yes, but remember there is *no dueling* in Ohio, for *any reason*." Charm says this with the peculiar emphasis that indicates there was another Incident. There's already been problems with a bank teller who didn't use her proper title and the HVAC guy who tried to give Prim his number and wound up with a nosebleed. "What should you do if you get in trouble?"

Prim sobers and recites, "Text you on the phone, like a normal person."

Her education in modernity is going pretty well, all things considered. Charm and me take her on lots of long walks through town, pointing out crosswalks and traffic patterns. We wasted an entire day in Pam's Corner Closet & More, explaining everything from fake fruit to microwaves. There have been some stumbling blocks (toilet paper, the internet, the whole concept of wage labor), but Prim is pretty sharp, it turns out, and I already knew she was brave.

In the evenings we tend to her cultural literacy by getting high and binging classic Disney movies and Austen adaptations (she agrees that the 2005 *Pride and Prejudice* is the superior version, because it is). Charm and Prim let me sit between them on the couch, my head on Charm's shoulder, my feet slung over Prim's legs, all our hands jostling in the popcorn bowl. It feels like all the slumber parties I never had growing up. It feels like a happy ending.

At Mom and Dad's it mostly feels like an endless party. Dad keeps baking cakes for no reason, humming off-key in the kitchen; Mom uses up all her vacation days at work, rather than hoarding them for some looming medical emergency; we reinstitute family game night and I discover, to my deep dismay, that Mom has been going easy on me in *Settlers of Catan* for twenty-one years. She straight-up stole my longest road without even a flicker of remorse.

I have the nagging sense that there are things I should be doing—applying for jobs or joining the Peace Corps or meditating on the profound gift of time—but all I seem to want to do is lounge around Roseville with everyone I love most.

It takes me a while to realize I'm saying goodbye.

I'm putting away groceries with Dad one evening when I pull a fresh set of twin sheets out of the bag, still wrapped in plastic. "Are these for me?"

Dad is halfway inside the fridge, rearranging Tupperware to make room for the milk. "They were half off! I figured you wouldn't want to take your old set with you. You've had them since what, middle school?"

I stare at the fridge door. "Am I . . . going somewhere?"

Dad reemerges with a pot of leftover lentils in one hand and limp celery in the other. He gives me a shrug and a smile that hangs a little crooked on his face, bittersweet. "You certainly don't have to. I guess it just felt like you might, now that you have . . ." He shrugs again. I consider all the ways he might have ended that sentence: a future, a life, a story still untold.

"Huh. Yeah. I guess." I feel it again, that sense of galaxies spinning around me, hanging like fruit ripe for the picking, and I know he's right. I stack diced tomatoes on the counter in silence before clearing my throat. "Would you and Mom be . . . okay, with that?"

He goes very still, a box of Cheerios in one hand.

"I mean, if I left for a while, maybe like a long while, you wouldn't freak out?"

Dad sets the Cheerios down and spreads his hands flat on the counter, his back to me. "When you disappeared, I thought that was it. Charmaine kept saying everything was fine, but I didn't really believe her. I thought maybe you'd run off, and that she was covering for you." His voice is low and thin, like he's forcing it through a tight throat. "It hurt like hell. Of course it did. I kept thinking about all the hours I spent trying to keep you here, trying to save you—or maybe myself—"

"Dad, I'm *sorry*—"

He slaps his palm on the counter. "And what a damn *waste* it was. Of my time, of our time together. I should have let you do whatever

the hell you wanted. I should have spent more time thinking about your life than worrying about your death."

He turns to face me finally, tears not merely gathering in his eyes but already sliding down his cheeks, pooling in the laugh lines around his mouth. He holds his arms out to me. "*I'm* sorry. Go wherever you want, with our blessing." I fall into him, stumbling over half-empty Save-A-Lot bags. "Just text sometimes, okay?"

The next morning I wake up with a slight headache from crying, a curious lightness in my chest, and a calm certainty that it's time to go. This time I pack the essentials: a few weeks' worth of meds, an alternate pair of jeans, my phone charger, my brand-new sheets, still in their plastic. A single splinter stolen from another world.

Mom's in the garden shaking junebugs into a pie pan of soapy water and Dad's sleeping in, so I leave a note beside the coffee maker. *Be back when I can. Expect me when you see me. Love, Zin.*

I'm in my car before I text Charm. Not on the groupchat we've been using for the last three weeks—on which we've finally convinced Prim to stop beginning every message with "To my Esteemed Companions Zinnia and Charmaine,"—but just her.

meet me at the tower, princess.

※ ※ ※

IT TAKES CHARM eleven minutes to get there, which is exactly the time it would take to read a text, pull on a pair of jeans, and drive from her place to the old state penitentiary. She must still be sleeping with her ringer on.

I raise a hand in greeting, leaning against the warm stone of the tower. She narrows her eyes at me, hair standing at wild angles, and stalks through the rutted dirt and overgrown grass to lean beside me.

She's close enough that I can feel the heat of her skin, see the rumpled pink lines the bedsheets left across her face. "Morning," I offer.

"Morning," she replies, coolly. "What the fuck?"

"Charm, please don't get upset—"

"If you ever speak to me in that tone of voice again, I will do crimes to you."

I should've known this would be way harder than leaving a note for my folks. I shut my mouth and fiddle with the wooden splinter in my hands. It's spent the last three weeks in my pocket, and the edges are already beginning to smooth with use. The end is still plenty sharp.

I feel Charm's eyes on my hands, hear the soft rush of her breath. "You're running, aren't you."

It isn't a question, so I don't answer it. I nod once to the ground.

"May I ask why?" Her voice is so carefully, ferociously calm, but I hear the bite beneath the calm, and the pain beneath the bite. "Why, now that you are magically healed, would you—"

I interrupt her in a soft, level voice. "I'm not healed. Not really." She already knows that. I showed her the little grayish blooms on the X-rays, my curse as-yet un-lifted. "All I have is more time."

She makes a surly, stubborn noise. "Which you could spend with *us*." I wonder if she realizes how quickly and tellingly her *me* has transformed into an *us*.

I don't look at her, speaking instead to the hazy green of the horizon. "I've spent every day since second grade with you, Charm, and I'm grateful for every second of it." I scuff my shoe against a dandelion, staining the earth yellow. "But even at the very best of times, there was a part of me that was just . . . playing out the clock. Waiting. Wishing I could save myself somehow, but never thinking I could aim higher."

"Higher?"

I clear my throat, wishing the truth was just a little less cheesy. "Saving others. I should have gone to all those stupid protests with Roseville's Children, I should have at least *tried*, and now it's too late." Last week a reporter from CNN asked to do a profile of me as "the oldest surviving victim of GRM." I never wrote back, but the word *victim* burrowed under my skin and itched at me, a brand-new allergy.

Charm doesn't say anything, so I keep talking to that green horizon. "I can't stop thinking about the others. Not just the other kids with Roseville's Malady, but the other sleeping beauties. The girls in other worlds who are dying or trapped or cursed, who deserve better stories than the ones they were given. Who are all alone." I run my fingertips across the point of the splinter and I know by the sharp sound of Charm's breath that she understands. That she sees the infinite pages of the universe turning before me, a vast book filled with a thousand wrongs that need righting, a thousand princesses that need rescuing, or at least a hand reached toward theirs in the darkness. "I don't know how much time I have, but I know what I want to do with it.

Charm exhales very slowly beside me. "And they said a folklore degree was impractical."

"Not if you're a cursed fairy tale princess, it turns out."

It's a weak joke, but Charm smiles for the first time since she stumbled out of her Corolla. "Maybe we got it wrong. Maybe you weren't the princess, after all. Maybe you're the prince." She rubs her Superman tattoo as she says it.

I shrug at her. "Or maybe we got the wrong story altogether. Maybe GRM is more like a poison apple than a curse, and there's seven dudes waiting to put me in a glass coffin when I die. Maybe my true love's kiss will revive me." I kick at the dandelion again. "Maybe there's a cure out there in one of those other worlds."

Charm gives me a sharp, sideways glance before squinting at the rising sun. "Nice to know you're trying to save yourself. Finally."

"Yeah, so maybe you can stop trying to save me. Finally."

I don't even have to look at her to feel the mulish set of her jaw. God, she's stubborn. I feel like I should warn Prim before I go. Then I remember the exclamation points and wonder if I should warn Charm instead. "Look, just—don't work for fucking Pfizer. Don't stick around Roseville. Go do something, anything else. Whatever you want. And take Prim with you."

"You are not the boss of me," Charm answers reflexively, but I can see the dangerous softening of her jaw at the mention of Prim's name. She swallows and adds, casually, "Hey, by the way: I love you." Her hands are jammed in her jeans pockets now, her eyes are still on the sky. "You don't have to say anything back—I know about your rules—I just thought you should know before you—"

I tip my head against her shoulder, right where Superman's hair curls against his forehead. "I love you, too." It's surprisingly easy to say, like the final tug that unties a knot. "It was a stupid rule."

"Hot, but stupid, like I've always said." Charm's voice is rough and gluey, full of tears again. "Will you come home? When you're ready?"

"Cross my heart."

"Okay." Charm turns and kisses me once, hard, on the top of my head. "I hope you find your happily ever after, or whatever."

"Already did," I say, and it's possible that my voice is a little gluey, too. "I'm just looking for a better once upon a time."

We don't say goodbye. We just stand for a while, my cheek still on her shoulder, watching the sun rise over Muskingum County. Eventually Charm sighs and walks back to her car. She turns and blows me a final, brassy kiss before she gets inside.

The tower still smells faintly of roses. I find them curling and drying in their buckets, their petals gathering in drifts against the walls. I watch Charm's car through the scummed windows, feeling the gathering heat of summer, thinking about stories that are told too often and the ink that bleeds from one cosmic page to the next and the stubborn arc of the universe. Charm's car vanishes around a bend in the road, sunlight flashing gold against the windshield, and then I'm a girl in a tower again.

But this time it's not midnight. This time I'm not drunk on despair and cheap beer, hoping desperately for a way out of my own story. This time, when I press my finger to the end of a splintered spindle, I'm smiling.

ACKNOWLEDGMENTS

IF WRITERS RECEIVED fairy blessings on their christening days, they couldn't hope for any better gifts than these:

An agent like Kate McKean, who has never met a tree she can't talk me out of.

An editor like Jonathan Strahan, who didn't laugh when I said I wanted to Spider-Verse a fairy tale, and an editor like Carl Engle-Laird, who is weak for the memes of the mid-2010s.

A publishing team like this one, including the patience, time, and talents of Irene Gallo, Ruoxi Chen, Oliver Dougherty, Troix Jackson, Jim Kapp, Lauren Hougen, Michelle Li, Christine Foltzer, Jess Kiley, Greg Collins, Nathan Weaver, Katherine Minerva, Rebecca Naimon, Mordicai Knode, Lauren Anesta, Sarah Reidy, Amanda Melfi, and everyone from Tor Ad/Promo. Expert consultants like Ace Tilton Ratcliff, who made this story smarter, kinder, and more true, and early readers like Ziv Wities, H. G. Parry, Sam Hawke, Rowenna Miller, Leife Shellcross, Anna Stephens, Tasha Suri, and the other denizens of the bunker, who all had better things to do with their time but spent it correcting my Tolkien references instead.

Friends like Corrie and Taye and Camille, who would break the laws of physics for me any day of the week.

Parents and brothers like the ones I have, who gave me my wonderful once upon a time.

And a partner and kids like the ones I found, who gave me my perfect happily ever after.